"Arabella, you must give me time."

"Time?" Ella inquired, conscious of his intense gaze. "What...sort of time?" she asked, wondering if he meant she should go away and return when it was more convenient.

"You must allow me time to know my subject," he said lightly, and Ella wasn't at all sure how she felt about that.

"Me, you mean?" she asked slowly, aware that she was playing for time.

His mouth curved upward. "Who else?"

Ella moistened her lip with the tip of her tongue—a nervous gesture. "How long will that take, do you suppose?" She suddenly felt flustered when that upward curve became a definite smile.

"A lifetime, I shouldn't wonder," he replied with such charm that all at once, Ella started to feel unexpectedly better about everything.

Jessica Steele first tried her hand at writing romance novels at her husband's encouragement two years after they were married. She fondly remembers the day her first novel was accepted for publication. "Peter mopped me up, and neither of us cooked that night," she recalls. "We went out to dinner." She and her husband live in a hundred-year-old cottage in Worcestershire, and they've traveled to many fascinating places—including China, Japan, Mexico and Hungary—that make wonderful settings for her books.

Books by Jessica Steele

HUNGARIAN RHAPSODY

Jessica Steele

Harlequin Books

TORONTO • NEW YORK • LONDON
AMSTERDAM • PARIS • SYDNEY • HAMBURG
STOCKHOLM • ATHENS • TOKYO • MILAN
MADRID • WARSAW • BUDAPEST • AUCKLAND

ISBN 0-373-03294-3

HUNGARIAN RHAPSODY

AUTHOR'S NOTE

Dear Reader,

My visit to Hungary was filled with many sights and sounds, and was over all too quickly. Budapest—a city divided by the Danube—is spanned by magnificent bridges and has much that I enjoyed. The architecture and monuments are splendid, but to dine to the accompaniment of haunting strains of gypsy music is a totally unforgettable experience.

I hope that I have been able to capture that experience for you in *Hungarian Rhapsody*. Enjoy!

Sincerely,

Jessica Steele

CHAPTER ONE

ELLA stared at her mother in disbelieving consternation as Constance Thorneloe ended, 'So there's nothing for it but that I shall have to cancel the trip.'

Her father, Ella decided, was not a very nice man. She loved him, of course, but that had nothing to do with it. He knew, he just *knew*, how very much her mother had been looking forward to their six-week tour of South America. Nevertheless, with the tour only five weeks distant, he had just telephoned—telephoned, mark you—from his City office to say he couldn't take so much time away from his work.

In Ella's view it was too bad of him. Yet here was her mother, ready to defend him. 'I suppose six weeks is a long time to be away from one's business,' Constance Thorneloe put her bitter disappointment behind her to state.

'But he never said anything at breakfast!' Ella protested, as ever amazed by her mother's sweet and gentle forgiving nature. With difficulty Ella swallowed down her ire, but as what her parent had said began to sink in. 'And you and Father haven't had a holiday in years!' she exclaimed crossly.

'I know dear, but...'

But nothing, Ella fumed. Her father was always pulling some stunt or other and she was fast coming to the conclusion that he had never intended to go on the South American holiday in the first place—and it was then that Ella metaphorically stuck her heels in. For it seemed to her, as she saw her hardworking mother's chance of doing something that would really please *her*, for a change, going down the drain, that it was about time that someone stood up to the master of Thorneloe Hall. And, as it came to her how over the years her father had appeared to take particular delight in upsetting one or other of them, the light of battle entered her brilliantly blue eyes. Her mother would cancel her much-looked-forward-to, needed, and *well-earned* holiday over her dead body!

'How would it be if I came with you in his place?' she asked, sternly holding down that she was furiously angry inside. Her mother would only feel she had to defend her husband if she let go with how she was feeling, but, in Ella's view, the way he had casually telephoned was indefensible.

'Would you?' All at once a wonderful beaming smile settled on her mother's refined features. 'Your father wouldn't mind, would he?'

'Of course he wouldn't!' Ella asserted stoutly, even as part of her wondered—Would he?

'Oh—but what about the shop?' Constance Thorneloe thought of one snag straight away.

Her mother was chief organiser of a charity shop in town. Since her husband would not sanction any daughter of his having 'a paid job', Ella, as well as helping her mother with the hundred and one other needy concerns she was involved with, helped out two days a week in the shop.

As evening approached, however, all snags had been ironed out. Ella's two very good friends Hatty Anvers and Mimi Orchard had rallied round and agreed to do a stint each in the shop for one day each week while they were away. Solutions had been found for any other minor problems too, so that all that remained, as mealtime arrived, was for someone to acquaint Rolf Thorneloe with the news of his replacement.

Rather than upset him before they began, Ella made a point of not being late down to dinner. Her brother, David, two years older and quiet and gentle like their mother, was already there when she entered the dining-room.

Dear David, she thought fondly, looking at her quiet-for-the-most-part brother. Where she and her father often struck sparks off each other, David was more likely to run a mile from a row, though he'd surprised them all about a year back when out of the blue he'd suddenly erupted. How the fur had really flown, she recalled, when David, his face ashen after having been shouted down, had insisted he should not be treated as a child.

'I'll treat you like an adult when you act in a grown-up and responsible way!' her father had roared and, as he had been insistent on finding fault with everyone, life generally at Thorneloe Hall had been unbearable for weeks afterwards.

'No date tonight, David?' she asked, hoping with all she had, for her sensitive brother's sake as much as any-one's, that there was not going to be any unpleasantness at the dinner table.

'She's washing her hair,' he joked, and Ella had an instinctive feeling that David, having a few times dated a girl she'd gone to college with, Viola Edmonds, would clam right up if she so much as asked him if he was very much smitten with Viola. 'The old chap's been in a good mood today,' said David, and he suddenly took her speculative thoughts from him and Viola, giving her something else to think about.

David worked for their father in his London office, so he would know. I know too, Ella thought, trying not to get angry. I'd like to bet he was in no end of a good mood, no end proud of himself after he'd put the phone down in the assumption that—not having to stir himself to go on holiday—he had put the kibosh on her mother's holiday hopes too. But not if she had anything to do with it.

Ella was again more than ready to take up cudgels on her mother's behalf when just then the dining-room door opened and both her parents came in. One look at her father's black-as-thunder expression, though, was all she needed to know that any good mood David had seen him in that day was a thing of the past. Clearly he was already acquainted with the news that her mother, rather than forgo the tour she had so eagerly looked forward to, had decided to go without him.

Ella sent her brother a telepathic 'Brace yourself, David, we're in for a rough mealtime', and took her place at the table. Her father, however, a dyed-in-the-wool traditionalist, and nothing if not a stickler for good manners—in front of the staff anyhow—had nothing to say until Gwennie—Mrs Gwendoline Gilbert, their housekeeper—had deposited a tureen of soup on the table, and departed.

Then, as Ella thought, Wait for it, he demanded, as though knowing that her mother would never have suggested it unaided, 'Was it your half-cocked idea, Arabella, that you should accompany your mother on this South American tour?'

You know jolly well it was, she fumed, always Arabella to him, her name never shortened. Refusing to glance her mother's way, knowing full well that her mother would be pleading with her with her eyes not to upset him further, Ella stared straight back at him. In her view, since he was so good at upsetting everybody else, it was about time somebody showed him that the world didn't revolve around him, and upset him for a change.

'Yes, it was,' she owned stubbornly, and dared, 'Though I fail to see what's so half-cocked about the idea!' She might have gone on, but her father, his expression looking blacker than ever, gave her no chance.

'It never occurred to you,' he went for her wrathfully, 'not for one unselfish moment, that with you and your mother gone your brother and I would have no one left to look after us!'

No one to look after them! Little short of amazed, Ella shot a glance to David. She saw at once from his bent head that he'd happily live on bread and cheese for the whole of six weeks—if only they'd stop arguing.

But it wouldn't come to that. Though rather than acquaint her father with the fact that they weren't living in the Middle Ages any longer, and that men had been known to cook a meal for themselves after a stint at the office, she quelled such rebellious thoughts, to answer quietly, 'I'm sure Gwennie will look after both you and David splendidly, the way she always has.'

Weathering her father's malevolent look, she fought hard for some more control. Gwennie had in fact been with them for as long as Ella could remember. But, while it was true that she and her mother sometimes practised their talents in the kitchen, in the main, and under the direction of her mother, Gwennie and the part-time staff had 'matters domestic' at the hall running like clockwork.

Ella was still staring stony-expressioned at her father when she saw something in his expression that warned, as perhaps she'd always known, that he wasn't so easily defeated. Yet, while she might have formed the view that he was carrying the old-fashioned principle of a woman's place being in the home much too far, she still couldn't see how he could deny that, with Gwennie and the rest of the staff there, he and his son would be as well-looked-after as ever.

'So you see,' she pushed on bravely, 'that there isn't any reason at all why Mother and I——'

'I've already told your mother that I wouldn't dream of spoiling her pleasure in this trip she has looked forward to for so long,' her father interrupted, and Ella felt wary—he was up to something! 'But,' he added, 'I've other plans for you, Arabella.'

Ella did not like the sound of this one little bit, but she was still determined that her mother was going to have her holiday —albeit alone—if absolutely necessary.

So, 'Oh?' she enquired, though had to wait a while for her answer when Gwennie came in to clear away soup that only the master had touched.

'You may recall,' Rolf Thorneloe resumed as soon as Gwennie had closed the door, 'that it's traditional for all the female Thorneloe offspring to have their portraits painted at the age of twenty-one. I think I may have mentioned it,' he tacked on with heavy sarcasm.

Had he ever! With her twenty-second birthday looming, it seemed to Ella that not a week had gone by when he'd not tried to hector her into agreeing to sit for the traditional portrait.

'Just because it's traditional, it doesn't necessarily mean that it's a good tradition,' she dug her toes in to reply, as determined then as she had been at the start not to have her portrait added to the positive staircase full of down-the-years twenty-one-year-old Thorneloe daughters there. Why she was being so determined—obstinate, her father called it—she couldn't have said. It wasn't as though she was ugly, or anything like that. Indeed, her thick and long red hair, pale complexion and fine features had been commented on as beautiful more than once. Perhaps the deep-down reason was from a growing desire not to give in to her father. She'd given in to him—no, been browbeaten by him—when, after initial ructions, she had for the sake of peace for everyone else finally had to consent to give up all idea of finding herself a job after college. Not that, as things had turned out, with her helping her mother so much, she'd have been able to find time to seek a career. But, that wasn't the point. 'Anyhow, I've more urgent matters to attend to than to sit for hours on end while some artist gets busy with oils and canvas,' she defended, not certain how she had come to be backed into a corner over this one.

'If taking a holiday with your mother is one of your "urgent matters", you can forget it!' And while Ella was about to say in contradiction that he was wrong and that the urgent matter she'd got in mind—for tomorrow anyway—was to help spruce up old Mr Wadcombe's cottage for when he came out of hospital at the end of the week, her father announced—with the air of a magician pulling off some stupendous trick, 'Through a mutual acquaintance, I was introduced to Zoltán Fazekas today.'

Ella's mouth fell open—this, was serious! 'Zoltán Fazekas, the—artist?' she asked, and suddenly found she was clinging desperately on to her determination not to have her portrait painted.

'The artist,' her father confirmed. 'He's in London for a few days on business. I was lucky enough to meet him—he's flying back to his home in Hungary tomorrow.'

That was a relief! Though, as she thought about it, and began to parcel together the stray bits and pieces her brain had retained from somewhere on the Hungarian artist, Ella started to relax. No way was a man of such artistic stature going to paint her. Although she seemed to have a wisp of a memory of reading he'd at one time done quite a bit of travelling to paint someone or other, she was fairly certain that he no longer did portraits. Wasn't his field landscapes these days?

Ella was still striving to find more from her memory when, to her utter amazement, 'I took the opportunity to ask him to paint your portrait,' her father stated brusquely.

'You've... My...' Flabbergasted, she stared at him in consternation, then rallied, keeping her fingers crossed in hope, as she challenged, 'But I didn't think he accepted commissions any more. I thought he was into landscapes—that sort of thing.'

'It's true enough that he has sufficient finance to please himself what he paints,' her father conceded grumpily. 'But he made his name painting portraits, so——'

'Well, there you are,' Ella butted in. 'It's unlikely that he'd agree to paint me. He hasn't agreed, has he?' she quickly asked, and then realising that her former determination had slipped quite badly, 'Not that it matters whether he has or he hasn't, I don't want my portrait painting and that's——'

'You're being tiresome,' her father cut her off, and, clearly having had enough of it, he went on to tell her that Zoltán Fazekas was a very busy man, and ordered her to stay put on the off-chance that the famous artist could fit her in with his schedule—and *that*, in her father's view, was *that*!

In other words, Ella fumed, while her father could not prevent her mother from going away on holiday, he had found one very good way of keeping one of the females of his family at home. Not that Zoltán Fazekas would be fitting her into his 'schedule'. Not in a million years would he.

The remainder of the meal was completed in silence—which was not unusual. Why her mother put up with it Ella couldn't think. If he were her husband she'd have strangled him years ago. Thinking of her mother, though, and how much she had to put up with, Ella suddenly grew positive again that her mother was going to have her holiday. She needed this holiday and, since it looked as though the block had been put on her accompanying her, Ella could see no reason whatsoever why her mother should not go alone.

She said as much the moment her father had gone off to the drawing-room with his after-dinner cigar. 'Do you think I should?' Constance Thorneloe asked, plainly the thought of going on her own never having occurred to her.

'Would you mind going on your own?' Ella countered.

'It would be—er—quite an adventure, wouldn't it,' her mother replied, but, from the sudden light in her eyes, Ella could tell that her mother was quite tickled by the idea.

'You're overdue for one,' Ella said softly, and, in a sentimental moment, she gave her parent a hug and a kiss.

The next day she scrubbed, cleaned and polished in old Mr Wadcombe's cottage, and planned to be a model daughter when her father was around. Not the slightest chance was she going to give him to try to prevent her mother's holiday. She was at the same time certain too that there was no way Zoltán Fazekas would find time—or inclination either for that matter—to paint her portrait, and felt that, had she given her father the impression she'd sit for Mr Fazekas, then she need take no steps to disabuse him of any such notion.

Her father made no mention of the 'portrait' at dinner that night. But, as though believing he had her consent over the issue, he appeared to feel able to afford to display his softer side, and actually asked how she had spent her day!

'I've been busy at Mr Wadcombe's cottage in the village,' she replied pleasantly, and when her father smiled benignly she was, as ever, amazed that he seemed to think that it was quite all right for her to labour like a slave provided the work was voluntary, yet would raise the roof if she so much as lifted a finger in paid employment.

'Are you going for your usual Friday night out with your crowd?' David asked her, looking somewhat cheered by the seemingly pleasant atmosphere around the dinner table.

'This Friday,' she replied lightly, having put to use a deal of her limitless energy in hours of solid slog, 'I'm for an early night!'

'Ironic, isn't it,' he laughed, 'that we pay Mrs Brighton to do our cleaning, yet here's you doing somebody else's for free?'

Their father was not amused by the comment, so Ella quickly changed the topic. She had an idea, however, that Mrs Brighton, who did their 'heavy' cleaning, would have walked out had she so much as caught a glimpse of the layers of dirt and grime, not to say filth, which Mr Wadcombe had nurtured over the years. Rubber gloves were a godsend!

By the following morning Ella was full of energy and with some to spare and drove over to the next village, as she did almost every Saturday morning, to help Jeremy Craven exercise the few horses his family kept. Jeremy was a year older than Ella and they were good friends and nothing more. Hatty Anvers, another of their group, drove up as they were rubbing the horses down, and talk between them drifted to the ball Hatty was having on her twenty-first birthday in six weeks' time.

'I seem to remember you had a mammoth coming-of-age party when you were eighteen,' Jeremy commented.

'What's that got to do with anything?' Hatty challenged.

'Nothing,' he quickly agreed—and they all burst out laughing. Ella drove herself home some while afterwards in a happy frame of mind.

A month later, she could hardly believe that over four weeks had gone by without a row at home. It was positively unheard-of for so much as a week to go by without her father finding fault with one of them. True, she had been on her best behaviour, she had to admit. And true, there had been some sore moments during mealtimes when her father had made some contentious remark, or expressed a view which she directly opposed, when she'd been hard-pressed to keep her silence. But, if keeping silent, and not rising to the most pointed and barbed comment, meant that her mother could take off for her South American tour this coming Saturday, it was a small price to pay.

Ella spent the next couple of days feeling as though she was treading on eggs whenever her father was in the house. Somehow there seemed to be tension everywhere when he was home, and it felt to her as if, things having gone on so smoothly for so long, one almighty row was just lurking in the background just waiting to explode.

Having determined, however, that any such row would not be instigated by her, she got up on Friday morning with her first thought being, Just twenty-four hours more to go and her mother would be away.

Breakfast went fairly well with Ella breathing a sigh of relief when her father went off to his office. By evening, though, expecting every moment something to go wrong, she would much preferred not to have gone down to dinner.

But, since not to present herself at the dinner table when she was neither dead, dying nor dining with friends would have most definitely caused her stickler-for-good-manners father no little irritation, she presented herself in the dining-room at the appropriate hour.

Her mother, she thought as she took her usual place at the table, was looking as tense as she herself was feeling. Ella knew then that, though too loyal to her husband to say a word against him, her mother too was living through the same fears and trepidation that she might yet, at this late stage, be called upon to cancel her much-looked-forward-to trip.

Ella sent her a warm smile, but knew better than to bring attention to the trip by asking the natural question that sprang to her lips—that question, 'All packed?'. Instead, she turned her attention to her father to enquire pleasantly, 'Did you have a good day at the office?'

'Particularly good,' he replied, so affably that Ella just knew he had either made a killing on the Stock Exchange—or he was up to something.

Not wanting to believe that, at this late stage, he was up to something that would prevent her mother from taking her holiday, 'Oh, you mean you've had a—er—fortunate day?' she enquired quietly.

'A most fortunate day, Arabella,' he beamed. And, when all her thoughts had been centred solely on her mother and the holiday she was going to ensure she took, he positively astounded her when he reiterated, 'Most fortunate,' and went on, 'I managed to contact Zoltán Fazekas by phone today—he has agreed to paint your portrait!'

She felt shaken to the core. Somehow, ridiculously, she then realised, she had not given the smallest thought of late to the subject of her portrait. Somehow, maybe because she had been so certain that Zoltán Fazekas would never agree to paint her, anyway, and she had had other things to think about, she had put the notion out of her head. But, astonishingly, here was her father saying that the Hungarian artist had agreed!

'Agreed?' she questioned, as all the objections she'd held before about the portrait welled in her again. She still wasn't certain why she objected so much. Yet it now seemed to her that a great principle was at stake. As though, with everyone having to give in so much to the law of her father, perhaps this was her way of sticking up for herself and her mother, and even, to some extent, her brother David.

'Agreed was what I said. Though not at first,' her father replied.

'Well, if you had to *persuade* him...' Ella began, feeling a tinge affronted, even if she did have no intention whatsoever of having the great Zoltán Fazekas—or anyone else—paint her.

'It was more that I had to agree that you'd fit in with his schedule,' her father cut in.

'You had to...' She played for time as she realised that, since her father didn't speak Hungarian, the Hungarian artist must speak English—well enough to communicate anyway—and wondered if she'd got the nerve to do a disappearing act. 'So, when's he arriving?' she thought she should find out for a start. But only to get shouted down by her parent for her trouble.

'He isn't arriving!' he exploded hotly. 'For heaven's sake, Arabella, where's your brain? He's one of the most talented artists living! You surely don't expect him to come to *you*! You should be highly flattered that——'

'But, if he isn't coming to me,' she butted in, certain with what knowledge she'd gleaned of the man that he was a man who travelled far and wide, 'how——?'

'*You* are going to *him*!' her father snapped.

'Where?' she asked incredulously.

'Hungary, of course!'

'Hungary?' she questioned, her lovely blue eyes going saucer-wide.

'Must you repeat everything I say?' Rolf Thorneloe retorted testily. 'Hungary's where you're going.' And, ploughing straight on as though she might try to butt in again, 'And, because he wants you where he can find you when the light is right, you're to spend the time it takes for him to complete your portrait in his home.'

'But...' She searched wildly for some sound form of protest, but she was in some small shock to have this *fait accompli* dropped on her, and the best she could initially come up with was, 'His wife won't want me as a houseguest.' And, warming to her theme, 'Why, the poor woman——'

'Zoltán Fazekas isn't married.'

Drat, she fumed impotently, but wasn't to be counted out yet. 'Then I can't possibly go and stay alone under his roof.'

'Don't be ridiculous!' her father retaliated shortly. 'Apart from the fact that you'll be more than adequately chaperoned by his household staff and your good upbringing, not to mention your own inherited moral fibre, Mr Fazekas has got better things to do than to try and seduce you.'

Mutinously Ella weathered the ticking-off from her father, but she still refused to knuckle under. So, knowing she was going to bring coals of wrath down about her head, 'And what,' she began to question stubbornly, 'if I decide I don't want to go?'

She thought she heard her mother suck in her breath as though the whole argument was painful to her. But Ella, in standing up to her father on this issue, even though she loved her mother so dearly, found that she just could not back down.

'That's quite simple,' he stated angrily. 'Either you go to Hungary—or I cut off your allowance.'

He would too, she knew it. 'So—I'll get a job!' Ella still refused to back down, even though she knew that she couldn't have said anything more guaranteed to outrage her father. Even though David sitting opposite, was looking as though he'd love to be many many miles away from the storm.

'I think you'll find, Arabella,' Rolf Thorneloe addressed her heavily, 'that neither I, nor your mother,' he added cunningly, 'will agree to that.'

And it was then, as Ella switched her glance from her brother to her mother, and saw the alarm, concern and defeated look in her mother's eyes, that she realised what she was doing. Stand up to her father she could, but not at the expense of her mother. For, somehow or other—and hadn't he, by bringing her mother into this, just said as much?—Ella knew that her mother was going to suffer for what he saw as her misdeeds.

Abruptly then the fight went out of her. That her father would cut off her allowance bothered her not one bit, but—and it had nothing to do with money—principles were all right if you could afford them. Ella knew then as she turned back to face her father that, of a certainty, she either agreed to go to Hungary or, as late in the day as it was, her mother could say goodbye to her South American tour.

'Couldn't you...?' She broke off, finding it terribly difficult to give in. 'Perhaps you could send Mr Fazekas a photo of me.' She tried to save her pride that that way she wouldn't actually be *sitting* for her portrait. 'Perhaps he could work from——'

'I've already sent him your photograph!' her father interrupted, and closed the subject to further conversation by stating sourly, 'You're going to Budapest—and that's an end to it!'

Ella lay in her bed that night fuming with impotent rage. She should have realised, she accepted belatedly, when up to a month ago not a week had gone by without her father making some reference to her wretched portrait, that just because he had fallen silent on the subject it didn't mean that he had forgotten it. Quite plainly he'd been hatching this ever since the last time the portrait had been under discussion.

She fumed some more when she realised exactly which photograph her father must have sent to Hungary. Oh, how she wished she had never given in when her father had said he wanted a picture of her and one of her mother for his desk. She'd thought then though, and been pleased at the thought, that, although he kept it well hidden, her father must care for them. Like a lamb she'd gone with her mother to the photographic studio.

Sleep was a long time claiming her that night. Though, before she eventually went to sleep, her father was not the only one to come in for some of her wrath. Why in creation did Zoltán Fazekas have to agree to paint her anyway? It wasn't as though he needed the money! You'd think he'd have something better to do!

There was no sign of anger about Ella when she drove her mother to the airport the next morning. If she was still feeling furious about the way she'd been manoeuvred into a corner then she concealed it under smiles and a show of light-heartedness, as she instructed her parent, 'Now forget about the lot of us and concentrate on you. Don't even send us a card if you don't feel like it.'

'Oh, I shall have to send you a card,' her mother replied, and Ella smiled, and hugged her tight—then said goodbye to her for six weeks.

She drove home knowing that she was going to miss her mother dreadfully but feeling much relieved that she was on her way. There had been times, most particularly last night, when that had been in grave doubt.

Sunday passed with Ella keeping out of her father's way as much as possible. She had no wish to quarrel with him, but she wasn't liking him very much at the moment.

Had she any hopes, however, that her keeping out of his way might see him forgetting their heated exchange of Friday evening, then she soon learned differently. For it was as she was about to leave the dining-room after dinner on Monday night that he said he would like to see her in his study for a few minutes.

Suspecting that what he wanted to see her about just had to be the portrait, she went with him to his study where he picked up a slip of paper from his desk, and handed it to her.

'This is Zoltán Fazekas's address and telephone number,' he told her, and while she was looking at it, 'I've transferred some extra funds into your account, and——'

'But I don't need any more money,' she protested.

'You will. Make your plane reservation as soon as you like,' he ordered.

Ella didn't like the sound of this one little bit, 'What about one of us—either Mother or me—having to stay home to look after you?' she pulled out of a thin nowhere.

'I'll survive,' he snapped.

Ella left his study telling herself that it was too late to make a flight reservation that night. Besides, no one took off—just like that. Having not given in to her father's instruction that night, though, by Tuesday a rebel had reared up in her and Ella was of the opinion that for her to go to Hungary, for goodness' sake, was preposterous.

It was as dinnertime approached on Wednesday evening, however, that something happened to make her wonder if it was so preposterous after all. She was coming down the stairs when she saw her brother below.

'How goes it?' she asked as he waited for her by the dining-room door. But she never got to hear his reply because just then the study door opened and their father, unsmiling and with his brow furrowed by thought, came out.

'Anything wrong, Father?' David asked him for his sins.

'I've no idea,' Rolf Thorneloe replied, 'but it looks as though I'm going to have to delay my dinner.' And, as both Ella and David looked at him expectantly, 'I've just had a phone call from Patrick Edmonds. He says he wants to come and talk to me on a most serious matter which apparently won't wait—he's on his way over. He...' A strangled sort of sound came from David, and both her father and Ella turned to stare at him.

'What's the matter, David?' Ella asked quickly—her brother was ashen!

'I...' He choked, coughed, then seemed to make an enormous effort to take a hold of himself, 'Viola—Mr Edmonds's daughter,' he paused to explain in case his father had forgotten, 'is—er...' he coughed again nervously ' ...is—pregnant.'

Oh, grief, Ella thought, no mistaking the fury on her father's face at what his intelligence had brought him.

'*What*?' he bellowed, clearly having forgotten nothing—and that included that his son had, several times recently, dated Patrick Edmonds' daughter. 'Dy you?' he demanded.

Ella saw David swallow; their father in a rage was never pleasant to see. But, 'Yes,' he owned bravely, and seemed to go paler still when Rolf Thorneloe's solution was immediate and denying any further discussion.

'She'll have to have an abortion!' he straight away decreed. But as Ella began to feel sick in her stomach and as ashen herself as David was looking, she discovered that her brother, when it mattered, was made of sterner stuff than he had ever before shown.

'No, she won't!' he faced his father to declare stoutly.

She saw that her father looked more than a little taken aback that his son could sound so determined. But, he had an answer for that too. 'Then you'll have to deny paternity!' he declared.

'I'll do nothing of the sort!' David erupted. 'Viola's a decent girl. She——'

'She sounds it!'

'She is!'

'You're not thinking of *marrying* her?'

'I would if she'd have me,' David retorted, his voice getting louder and louder all the time, 'but she won't!'

'You must be off your head!' Rolf Thorneloe was in full throttle when just then Gwennie hove into view. That one look at the scene was sufficient for her to do a swift about-turn and go back the way she had come, was of no consequence when, 'My study!' he ordered, and he and his son went storming in that direction. Ella took a couple of steps after them, but her father's closing the study door firmly in her face gave her a fair hint that her presence was not required.

Had her brother remained the same barely-a-word-out-of-place brother she had always known, then Ella felt she might well have gone and opened the study door anyway. But, as all hell sounded as though it was breaking loose behind that door, her brother's voice every bit as loud as her father's, Ella realised that her assistance was not required. Hadn't David just very clearly shown that, when anything mattered to him sufficiently he was quite capable of taking care of himself without any help from her?

She turned towards the dining-room but found that she had no appetite whatsoever, so she turned to the stairs, unconscious of the portraits of the Thorneloe women staring down at her as she started to climb.

Patrick Edmonds must be furious about his daughter, she reflected as she paused near the top of the wide staircase. But, judging by the strains of the row going on in the study reaching her ears from where she stood, he couldn't be any more furious than her father was about his son.

She recalled some of her father's past moods, which had gone on for weeks, and realised gloomily that life at Thorneloe Hall looked like being absolute hell for some time to come. What she needed, she mused, as her gaze absently fell on the descending line of portraits, was a bolt-hole of some sort.

That was when she suddenly became aware of the oil-paintings she had been staring at without really seeing them. Now, how about that for an idea? Ella was deep in thought when she turned her feet in the direction of her room.

But she did not need to think for long. By the time she'd reached her door she had remembered how, only minutes ago, David had emerged before her eyes as a man. Certainly he was man enough to make Viola pregnant. All things considered, Ella decided that her brother had shown himself man enough not to need to have her around to absorb some of her father's flak.

With that knowledge Ella turned about, a plan forming as she made for her mother's room where, her plan gathering momentum, she quickly set about removing from her mother's desk all papers pertaining to the South American tour. Her father might believe that everything in the home pivoted around him, she mused, which it did to a great degree. But, in moments of crisis, it was to Constance Thorneloe with her quiet inner strength that they looked—her husband included. Since Ella had got her mother away on holiday, there was no way her father was going to call his wife home, she decided.

From her mother's room, Ella then went to the library and searched amongst the modern additions until she located a guide book on Eastern Europe which, as well as listing airlines, also listed hotels. Shortly afterwards she was back upstairs and finding it most useful to have a telephone in her room.

One out of two wasn't bad, she considered some minutes later when, having had no luck in contacting MALÉV, the Hungarian airline, she had by dint of a call to Budapest, and an English-speaking reservations clerk, been able to make a hotel reservation commencing the following night. Deciding to ring the airline as soon as they opened in the morning, she then turned her attention to her packing. It was with some reluctance, though, that with her suitcase packed, she had to get out another one when she only by the merest chance realised that—because of tradition—she'd have to pack a ballgown to be painted in.

By morning, however, all that was left to do was to make a few phone calls—and to endure breakfast. Had either her father or David been more communicative over that breakfast then Ella felt she might have given them some hint of her plans for that day. But, with breakfast taken in a freezing atmosphere that could have been cut with a knife, neither of the male Thorneloes had a word they wanted to impart before they made their way to the City.

'David!' she impulsively followed him to call after him as he left the house, but his head must have been filled with his own thoughts, for he did not hear her. She let him go, went glumly to ring the airline, and she was informed that there was a flight with a seat available at lunchtime that day. All that remained then was for her to ring her friends Hatty and Mimi, and to tell them that she'd like to take up their previous agreement to work in the shop—then she hared off to pick up her flight ticket.

It was with mixed feelings that she boarded her plane and, later, booked into her hotel in Budapest. It was then, though, that, having got there, she had space to take stock and wonder—what in creation was she doing here? Was Budapest, in fact, the lesser of the two evils? She then recalled the frosty atmosphere at her home that morning, and supposed it was—but she still didn't want her portrait painting!

Realising that she was starving, she decided to go in search of the hotel's restaurant. Then she recollected how she'd put her watch on an hour to Hungarian time, and supposed, since her father would be expecting her to dine at Thorneloe Hall, that she'd better get busy with her telephone dialling finger.

'Where?' he asked in amazement when she told him where she was.

'I'm in Hungary. I thought you wanted me to come here,' she added, just in case he'd forgotten the fuss he'd made about it.

'I hope you gave Mr Fazekas more notice than you've given me!' he complained, after barely a pause, and, at the sudden silence from the other end, 'You *are* in Mr Fazekas's home?' he abruptly demanded, and stung her ears some more when she told him that she had booked herself into a hotel. 'You know damn well he's expecting you!' her father ended. 'Ring him at once, tell him you've arrived—and *don't* forget to apologise!'

Apologise! What for? 'Yes, Father,' she murmured, and would have said her goodbyes had he not quickly found something he wanted to ask.

'Where the hell's your mother staying? You must know. I can't find her itinerary anywhere.'

'This is a dreadful line,' Ella at once invented, and put down the phone to have a dreadful tussle of conscience about the South American papers she had 'lost'.

A few minutes later she felt that she had been right to do what she had. An unexpected feeling of guilt caught her out, however, and guilt, she discovered, was a hard taskmaster. So that, even though she'd initially had no intention whatsoever of ringing Zoltán Fazekas that evening, the exhumed guilt at removing her mother's itinerary, and the love she had for her father, despite the tyrant he was, saw her finding the piece of paper she'd brought with her, and dialling once more.

'Hello,' she said evenly when, her call answered, a very masculine voice said something Hungarian and completely incomprehensible to her. 'I would like to speak with Mr Zoltán Fazekas, please,' she enunciated very slowly, and hoped that whoever was on the other end had a smattering of English.

'You're speaking with him,' he answered, far from having only a smattering of English, sounding, with barely a trace of accent, completely at home with her language.

'Oh, good,' she replied more swiftly, and, knowing that her father would never have shortened her name, mouthful that it was, 'My name is Arabella Thorneloe,' she informed him. 'I'm in Budapest—I believe you're expecting me?' The silence that greeted her announcement caused her to wonder if perhaps his English was not as good as she'd thought. But, since he wasn't offering anything in either Hungarian or English, she tried again, this time going on to tell him of the name of her hotel. And when that brought forth no comment either, she tried one last time by asking the question, 'Was I supposed to come to you?'

This time, he did reply, but in such a way that she was left staring, disbelievingly at the telephone in her hand, for, 'You'll come to no harm where you are,' he clipped, and, while she was taking that in—he actually put the phone down on her!

CHAPTER TWO

ELLA was still thinking an aggrieved 'Well!' at Zoltán Fazekas's clipped manner and attitude when she took her bath the following morning. If he was as curt in his own language as he was in English, then was he a barrel-load of charm!

She emerged from the bathroom realising that, having given in about her portrait—it seeming the lesser of two evils when she'd caught the plane yesterday—she was committed to spending lord knew how long residing with some crusty old bachelor.

Not that he'd sounded all that old. Mature, certainly, but, from the remembered crisp and alert tone of his voice, Ella on second thoughts suspected that she could do away with any idea that he was in his dotage.

She went down to the hotel's restaurant, and was breakfasting on a bread roll and some cheese when it occurred to her that she hadn't been all that smart to take flight until the period of unpleasantness had waned at home. Though, as she toyed with the idea of going back, she realised on reflection that, since it seemed she had somehow—if not actually by word of mouth— agreed to her father's 'Have your portrait painted or else' dictate, she had better stay where she was. That or risk yet more unpleasantness, not to say out-and-out spleen-ishness, should she return to England 'unpainted'. In any event, she shuddered, it would be absolute murder at home until the dust had settled on poor David's up-setting the apple cart.

She winced at the thought of the dreadful atmosphere at Thorneloe Hall, and abruptly shied away from all idea of returning there in a hurry. Most decidedly, she considered, since she was here in Zoltán Fazekas's country now, to stay did seem to be her best plan. The only problem there, though, was that Zoltán Fazekas did not appear to give a damn where she was! Well, she'd be hanged if she'd ring him again!

Having sorted out in her head that, although it went against the grain, she would stay in Hungary and have her portrait painted, she returned to her room to collect a top coat. She had no intention of sitting around just waiting to be summoned by the artist, but had no intention either, since it was a cold grey day outside, of freezing to death as she walked around exploring the Hungarian capital. She found that she was quite looking forward to taking a look at the city which was divided by the river Danube, with the Buda hills on one side and Pest and the beginning of the Great Plain on the other.

She had just picked up her handbag after shrugging into her coat, however, when her telephone rang. Dropping her bag to the bed, she went to answer it. 'Hello?' she enquired.

'Presumably you can make it here unaided?' a male voice clipped, a male voice which she recognised straight away, for all she had only heard it once before.

For some reason, just his attitude annoyed her. 'What?' she questioned.

'Check out of your hotel and come to me!' he demanded, and Ella bristled some more. Who the dickens did he think he was with his orders? She hadn't yesterday taken herself out of the jurisdiction of one tyrant only to put herself under the bossy influence of another! 'You have my address?' he questioned sharply when she was too slow in answering.

'I have, but——' It was a waste of time thinking that she would tell him that she intended to do a little sight-seeing first, she found, because, quite unceremoniously, he chopped her off.

'The sooner we start, the sooner we finish!' he cut in curtly, and, as before, he again put down the phone on her.

Well, really! she fumed, but wasn't sure then which infuriated her more—his despotic attitude, or the fact that he had just as good as told her that he couldn't wait to be rid of her—and he hadn't even met her yet!

Well, he could go and take a running jump for a start! She wasn't rushing around doing anyone's bidding. On that mutinous thought Ella left her hotel room and, taking a look at the facilities the hotel had to offer, she changed some sterling for some Hungarian forints, and then, taking her time, she went and selected a dozen or more picture postcards to send home. She then went and found a seat in the lounge, and, unconscious of admiring glances, she wrote cards to distant aunts and uncles, to Gwennie and also to Mrs Brighton, and to the rest of the staff at Thorneloe Hall. As well as sending cards to all her friends, she wrote a card to her brother and to one tyrant of her acquaintance, her father. The other tyrant, not yet encountered in person, was, though, she disconcertingly discovered, never far from her thoughts.

All her cards were written and posted when she was having a delaying cup of coffee in the hotel's coffee-shop. She found, however, that she was too churned up inside to sample one of the delicious-looking pastries on display. Zoltán Fazekas was at the root, of course. Though how it came to be that she had let the man get to her so, when she had not so much as clapped eyes on him, was beyond her.

Ella finished her coffee, but she was stubbornly still not yet ready to do his bidding, when she remembered old Mr Wadcombe, out of hospital now and doing well, though he'd been a bit down when she'd visited him last week. It might cheer him a little to receive a picture postcard from Hungary.

Later, having selected another postcard, written it and posted it, Ella returned to her room and took a shower. After her shower she brushed her long and luxurious thick red hair and applied the small amount of make-up that she normally wore, and donned a classic burnt amber suit of lightweight wool, then began to put her belongings together. Then she phoned down and asked the desk captain to send a bell-boy to her room for her luggage, and went down to reception to settle her account.

On the stroke of midday, with her top coat draped over her shoulders, Ella stepped into a taxi that would take her to the home of one Zoltán Fazekas. She was not normally a nervous person but as the taxi raced through traffic—perhaps they didn't have speed-limits in Hungary—she admitted to something akin to butter-flies in her tummy, yet knew it had nothing to do with the speed merchant she happened to have for a driver.

Zoltán Fazekas's home was in an exclusive area of the Buda hills, Ella realised, as the taxi driver pulled up and took her cases to a smart front door. 'Köszönöm,' she thanked him, in the only piece of Hungarian which she had so far managed to pick up—and brought a flurry of Magyar down on her head as he thanked her pro-fusely for her generous tip.

Having no idea what he'd said, her only option was to invoke the international language of a smile. So she smiled, and he beamed, but went on his way, and Ella turned her attention to the doorbell. A stocky lady of

firm proportions, dressed neatly in navy, answered her
ring, '*Jó napot*,' she greeted her dourly. But while Ella
hoped she was saying 'Good afternoon and was hoping
to make herself understood, the woman looked to her
cases, murmured a universal 'Ah', and, to let her know
she was expected, opened the door wider and, with a
call of 'Oszvald!', a flow of words left her, of which Ella
understood not one.

The woman's gesture that she step over the threshold,
was understood, however, as was her, '*Nem, Oszvald*,'
when the woman gestured that she should leave her
luggage where it was. Presumably, Oszvald was coming
for it. A short, similarly stocky man, of around the same
mid-fifties age as the woman, appeared just as Ella entered the thickly carpeted hall. Oszvald, she guessed when
on some instruction from the woman he went straight
to her cases and brought them in, then, passing her with
a pleasant '*Jó napot*,' he headed further up the hall to
a wide staircase.

'Do you by any chance speak English?' Ella asked the
woman, but had her answer in the blank look that met
her words.

Ella wondered if the woman was the housekeeper, but,
with no sign of Zoltán Fazekas about, there was no one
she could ask. Though, since Oszvald had waltzed off
with her cases, she reckoned she could safely presume
that she had come to the right address. And the woman
went to the stairs and, it being plain by then that she
wanted to show her to her room, Ella went with her.

The house was over several floors, she observed, but
the room the woman took her to was on the first floor,
and Ella saw she could have nothing to complain of
about her room. It was thickly carpeted in cream, had
just a hint of pink in the colour of the walls, with a
plump pink duvet on the large bed and excellent richly

mahogany furniture. There was another door in the room which the woman went over and opened to reveal an adjoining bathroom, then let go with a stream of something entirely incomprehensible as far as Ella was concerned.

'I'm sorry,' she began to apologise, and discovered that there were plenty of ways around a language barrier when the woman came and showing her watch, pointed to two o'clock.

'*Ebéd*!' she stated, and gave her watch another tap.

'*Köszönöm*,' Ella replied pleasantly, and was quite happy to be left alone when the woman departed so that she could try and work out what was to happen at two o'clock.

Clearly, for all Zoltán Fazekas had ordered her to 'Check out of your hotel and come to me!' the artist wasn't home. Oh, crumbs, she did so hope he wasn't one of the temperamental sort who went into a huff when one didn't fly to obey his commands. She had no idea how long it took to have one's portrait painted, but began to hope then that it would take days rather than weeks— though she still had no wish to return home until things had quietened down. Meantime, did *ebéd* mean something to do with the master coming home—or something else?

At a few minutes before one Ella left her room and went downstairs to the hall below. She had hoped that the housekeeper, if housekeeper she be, might hear her and think to come looking.

Ella realised that she had the density of the carpet to thank for the fact that her footsteps were muffled. But, on seeing that one of the many doors leading off the wide hall was opened the merest crack, she went and pushed it inwards, and found herself in a comfortable, tastefully furnished drawing-room.

Her stomach had been hoping she might find a dining-room, but, as she seated herself in a commodious arm-chair, she relaxed and resorted to whimsy. Perhaps no one ate lunch at Zoltán Fazekas's home. Perhaps they didn't eat dinner either. Perhaps he didn't even have a dining-room.

At half-past one, with no sign of food, or anyone else, Ella was beginning to wish that she'd forced down a pastry with her coffee. She toyed briefly with the idea of going out and having a bite to eat somewhere but, on reflection, decided against the notion. It was her own fault, by refusing to comply with Zoltán Fazekas's bossy, intimated 'Come at once' edict, that she had missed seeing him—not that she regretted her delaying tactics. But since she had an idea that he'd be home at two, her basic good manners surfaced to suggest that it wouldn't hurt her to stay put for another half an hour.

At ten minutes to two, Ella left the comfort of her chair, and, keeping a discreet distance so she should not be seen from the street, she went to look out of the window.

Straight-backed and slender in her burnt-amber suit with its hemline ending just above the knee, she con-centrated her eyes on all who walked about, trying to decide which if any of the males might be her host ar-riving home. He might well arrive by car, which was more than likely, she mused, but was just contemplating the bent-over figure of a very slight man, when a sudden sound behind her made her spin round.

Zoltán Fazekas, if this be he—and she was sure it was—was neither bent over nor slight, but tall; a man somewhere in his mid-thirties, he was powerfully built but without spare flesh—and quite something! My stars, Ella thought faintly, as the cool grey eyes of the dark-haired man unhurriedly took in her every feature and then travelled over her mass of shining red hair, down over her form to take in her long shapely legs and on down to her smartly clad feet, was he ever *something*!

Having felt too stunned to move, however, she found herself going forward when, his inspection of her completed, he extended his right hand. 'Zoltán Fazekas,' he stated formally, the feel of his touch as cool as his un-smiling look yet, at the same time, burning, as he shook hands with her.

'Arabella Thorneloe,' she murmured, unnecessarily, she knew, but, as she took on board that this man did not like her, she suddenly felt a need to say something.

'I hope you're happy with your room,' he showed himself a perfect host to comment. 'You must ask Frida if you have not all you require.'

'Frida?' she asked, unable to refrain from tilting her chin an uppity fraction—she was unused to being dis-liked on sight.

For a cool moment he stared at her, nothing lost on him, she was all at once sure. Then, 'My housekeeper,' he deigned to reply.

'The lady who let me in?'

He nodded. 'Frida doesn't often disturb me when I'm working,' he informed her, and Ella guessed from that that the roof would most likely have to fall in before she would dare.

Though, if he had been working, did that mean that he had a studio in the house somewhere? That, in fact, he had been in the house the whole time? And, if that be so, then what the heck was this *ebéd* which his house-keeper had referred to? Ella thought it might be an idea to find out.

'What does *ebéd* mean?' she enquired, but on looking at her host she found that there was something about the man that caused her to have the utmost difficulty in remembering how very cross Zoltán Fazekas and his bossy telephone instructions had made her.

'Lunch!' he clipped in explanation.

Ella discovered a need to glance away from his cool grey eyes. She took a glance at her watch—it was as near two o'clock as made no difference. 'Good,' she announced flatly, 'I'm starving.'

It was him, everything about him, she decided, for she was certain that she had never met anyone at all like him, that made her say things which she would never normally say. The way she'd been brought up, good manners a priority on the list, she should have been prepared to fade away rather than own to hunger while a guest in someone else's house! Realising that she had better apologise, she flicked a glance to her host, and promptly forgot any such apology. For, though it was quickly controlled, she could have sworn that his mouth—a rather nice mouth, she had to own—had briefly quirked up at the corners.

She was still feeling startled that anything she had said could possibly have resulted in a slight lessening of his stony expression, when, 'If you'd like to come with me, I'll get you fed before you pass out on me,' he suggested.

'Your English is excellent.' She again found her tongue running away with her as she preceded him out into the hall. He did not thank her—she hardly expected him to—though as he touched a hand to her elbow to point her in the direction she was to go, fearing he might counter 'How's your Hungarian?' she abruptly asked, 'Who's Oszvald?'

'Frida's husband,' he answered, and had nothing more to say as he escorted her to an elegant dining-room where Frida was waiting to serve them.

Ella took the seat which Zoltán Fazekas pulled out for her before he went and took his own seat opposite, then Frida, as unsmiling as ever, came to ladle soup into her bowl.

Heaven save us, what a grim household, Ella thought, as the housekeeper served her master. Though when she flicked a glance to them both as the artist made some commont to the woman, Ella was surprised to see that the housekeeper could *actually* smile—and that the master did at least look pleasant when he addressed his staff.

Well, isn't that ducky? she thought, irritated. Feeling most definitely disliked and unwanted in his household, she wondered why Zoltán Fazekas had consented to paint her in the first place. A moment later, as the housekeeper left the room, Ella was certain that she didn't care a light anyhow; she'd never wanted to come here to start with. Though since, in all honesty, she didn't feel that her home in England was the place to be right now either—she was rather stuck for choice.

'Is the soup to your liking?' her host's voice suddenly broke through her thoughts, causing her to wonder if he thought it odd that she should declare herself starving yet take barely a spoonful of what was in front of her. It surprised her that he had noticed, though.

'It's delicious,' she replied, which was no more than the truth, and took another spoonful, then enquired, 'What is it?'

'*Jókai bableves,*' he answered, and translated, 'Bean soup,' going on to enlighten her further. 'It is named after Mór Jókai, who was one of Hungary's most prolific and popular writers.'

Ella tucked into the remainder of her soup, quickly forming the opinion that the housekeeper was quite something of a cook into the bargain. Whatever her private thoughts about her welcome, however, it seemed to her that, since her host had opened up to be more than monosyllabic, that as his guest, she could observe the courtesies too.

'Do you have your studio on these premises?' she enquired, as she finished the last of her first course, and laid down her spoon.

'The whole of the top floor has been converted to a work-room,' he replied easily, and, as the housekeeper came in and served the next course of meat and vegetables, he had nothing more to say.

'You've been working this morning, I think you said,' Ella resumed as she cut into a potato.

'There's always something to do, don't you find?' he countered.

Why did she feel that they were, in some way, fighting? she wondered as she carried on with her meal. Somehow she had a feeling that Zoltán Fazekas had been anti Arabella Thorneloe from before they'd met.

Well, that was fine by her, she thought proudly; she wasn't too gone on him either. 'Do we begin work this afternoon on my portrait?' she asked him, a shade acidly, she had to own. And, for her pains, had to suffer a lengthy scrutiny from those cool grey eyes.

Purely because he was an artist, she suffered his long exploration of her face, but, from that suffering, she found *him* quite insufferable when he shook his head, and then drawled, 'You look tired.'

'Thanks,' she retorted tartly, was immediately half inclined to apologise for her waspish tone, then thought, Why in blazes should she?

While a part of her, a logical part, said that she was being over-sensitive and that she shouldn't let personalities enter into what, after all, was only a job she had come to have done—a very professional job, admittedly, and by an expert in that field—there was a part of her that, for some unknown reason, could not help but be affected by personalities. She wasn't used to being disliked on sight. She wasn't used to anyone being anti Arabella Thorneloe. And if he was an artist anywhere near half as good as his fame, she'd have thought he'd have the expertise to paint out any mauve shadows from beneath her eyes. Or, for that matter, not paint them in in the first place! And, for starters, she'd never jolly well wanted her picture painted anyhow!

Good manners or no good manners, Ella had started to feel so incensed about this artist who would apparently only be truthful to his art that she felt she had nothing further she wanted to say to him. The same, she guessed, went for him, because any pretence of harmonious host and guest relationship had totally disappeared—if it hadn't only been a figment of her imagination anyway—and the rest of the meal was completed in cool silence.

Zoltán Fazekas was much in Ella's head when that afternoon she got busy with her unpacking. It annoyed her, particularly annoyed her, that, when she didn't want to think of him at all, she should remember the way he looked, the nice, not to say superb shape of his mouth, once—she'd been crass enough to believe—with a trace of a smile upon it. The man might have an artist's eye as he studied her long and hard over lunch—no, over *ebéd*—but it would please her mightily if he'd get on with it.

He had every right not to like her on meeting her, she fairly, if mutinously allowed, but he had no right whatsoever to prejudge her before he'd even seen her. And, to be anti her, sight unseen, must mean he had prejudged her. For a minute or so she wondered if her father had said something to him which had caused him to form an adverse opinion of her. But, after a minute of thinking about it, she knew that, whatever else her father was or was not, he was totally loyal to his family to outsiders.

Being unable to come to any conclusion why Zoltán Fazekas should—in advance—have such a down on her, Ella grabbed up an armful of clothes that had travelled badly and, pleasantly hoping that Zoltán Fazekas ran out of whatever colour he was using that afternoon, she left her room.

Anticipating that at this hour Frida, if she was anything like Gwennie, would be either out following her own pursuits or putting her feet up in her own apartments, Ella went in search of the kitchen. She found it after a couple of false starts, and once inside also found the door that led into the laundry-room.

Her thoughts were again mutinously on her host as she ran an iron over first one article and then another. It irked her more than somewhat that, having presented herself in Hungary to have her portrait painted, the artist should not yet be ready to paint her.

Ella might have grown yet more mutinous, but just then her inherent streak of fairness again chose to annoyingly surface. Was it likely he'd drop everything the moment she arrived, for goodness' sake? A man of his artistic reputation!

By the time she was pressing the last item of clothing, she had simmered down considerably and was forming the view that perhaps she was expecting too much. At fault of course lay Zoltán Fazekas's curt 'The sooner we start, the sooner we finish' of that morning.

Ella had just decided that he must have meant for her to use today to settle in at his home ready for him to start work tomorrow when suddenly Frida bustled into the kitchen, and on seeing her in the laundry-room— looked quite horror-stricken.

For a second or two Ella was quite mystified when, with a veritable stream of Hungarian, the housekeeper hurried forward pointing to herself.

'I'm sorry,' Ella apologised, realising that somehow she had done something wrong.

A minute later, however, by means of much sign language, Frida pointing to the iron and then herself again, then pointing to the pile of ironing Ella had just completed, and then back to herself again, Ella got the gist of what the housekeeper was trying to convey.

'It's all right,' Ella smiled, and laughed a little to herself because no way was the good lady going to understand. 'I—do,' she added, pointing smilingly to the ironing.

'*Nem*!' the housekeeper replied, and, pointing to herself, 'Frida,' she said, making ironing motions.

Ella gave it up. '*Köszönöm*,' she smiled, and, carefully scooping up her recently pressed garments, was about to return to her room when she saw that Frida was pointing to her watch.

'*Vacsora*!' she said pointing to eight o'clock, and actually smiled.

'*Köszönöm*,' Ella repeated, and felt fairly confident, as she left the kitchen, that dinner would be at eight o'clock.

When at seven forty-five that evening she was ready to go downstairs to dinner, Ella realised that the small but friendly exchange with the housekeeper had lightened her mood. She felt in much better spirits than she had, anyhow, she mused, as she checked her appearance in the mirror. She had showered and changed into a blue short-sleeved elegant dress of jersey wool, and was quite pleased with the result. She was just turning away from the mirror, however, when someone came and tapped on her door.

She went and opened it, and 'Oh—hello!' she exclaimed, and at once felt ridiculous that she should be so surprised to see Zoltán Fazekas standing there — it was his house, for goodness' sake. My word, though, was he *something*, she couldn't help thinking again of the man who, in a dark suit of impeccable cut, stared down into her startled blue eyes.

'I should have told you—dinner is at eight,' he offered pleasantly, this clearly being the reason for his call, and, while Ella felt her heart skip a ridiculous nonsensical little beat that he could be both 'quite something' *and* pleasant with it, a thought which put her off her stride, he continued, 'Are you ready?'

Ella went down the stairs with him and, strangely, she felt more aware of him than of any man she knew. She was sharing a pre-dinner drink with him when she realised that it was only because he was taller than most of her male friends that she had felt the way she had when walking down the stairs with him.

'Frida tells me you have been busy in the domestic regions of the house,' he commented when they were seated in the dining-room and the housekeeper came in to serve the soup.

'She wasn't offended that I made free with her iron?' Ella asked, as the housekeeper smilingly attended to her soup dish.

'You can be certain she was not,' he replied, his glance going from one to the other. 'My housekeeper is normally most reserved with her smiles.'

I wonder from whom she takes her lead? Ella thought wryly, so far only ever having glimpsed once the barest trace of a smile on his countenance—and not being too certain about that one. Though, since he was being pleasant, she endeavoured to be the same, and the meal progressed to the next course.

'This is quite delicious,' Ella felt she could do no other than comment as she took one and then another forkful of the plates of various meats set before her, tasting onion, tomato and green pepper too. 'Does it have any special name?' she wanted to know.

'It'o called *hét vezér tokány*—seven chiefs' *tokány*,' he obliged.

'Named after seven chiefs?' she enquired.

'I can see you're no empty-headed redhead,' he commented, and, while she was busy wondering if he was being complimentary, he indulged her curiosity. 'Named, as you've rightly guessed, after seven chiefs, the chiefs of the seven Magyar tribes who, at the end of their migrations, settled in the Carpathian Basin.'

Ella had a natural thirst for knowledge and, her appetite whetted, other questions about his countrymen sprang to mind. But Zoltán Fazekas was pouring her a glass of wine, and her curiosity was born about something else, 'This is a Hungarian wine, isn't it?' she questioned and taking a sip, was quite impressed with the quality of the *Villányi kadarka*.

'We have quite a wine industry in my country,' he informed her, and Ella began to be quite struck by how pleasant he could be—when he wasn't being the reverse.

Ella's opinion about how pleasant he was being underwent a rapid change, however, by the time she was spooning into her dessert. It was perfectly natural, she felt, that she should need to know what time he would require her to present herself at his studio in the morning. So she didn't believe that she had any need to think twice before she put her question to him.

So, 'What time would you like me to come up in the morning?' she enquired during the tiny lull that followed a brief discussion on the music of the Hungarian composer Bartók.

'Come up?' her host enquired, his tone she felt, most definitely cooler.

'Presumably, you wish me to sit tomorrow!' she stated, her own tones none too warm, she had to confess.

'Sit?' he questioned yet again—and that made her cross.

He was as at home with the English language as she, she knew darn well he was! 'You said, and I quote,' she reminded him as evenly as she could, 'that the sooner we start on my portrait, the sooner we finish.'

'You have some urgent need to get back to England?' he questioned toughly, all sign of pleasantness vanished. 'Some man friend, perhaps?' he barked.

Astonished by his sudden change of mood, his sudden attack, Ella blinked as she wondered how men friends had got into this! But, while thinking, Heaven save me from temperamental artists, she strove to stay calm. 'I have many friends,' she then told him after a few moments. 'Some of whom happen to be men. But, there's no one man in particular that I...' She broke off when it became apparent from his expression that he didn't want a long and boring diatribe for an answer. Further, that he wasn't more than interested in passing anyway—which he showed by asking an entirely different question—though still on the theme of her wanting to rush back to England.

'You have a career, a job of work which you cannot take too much time from?' he enquired.

'I don't have a career, a job,' she replied. 'My father...' She broke off again when she realised that he couldn't possibly be interested in the fact that her father had forbidden her to do paid work.

Though she was quite unprepared for her host's cool, 'In Hungary, people have two, three and sometimes as many as four jobs.'

From that, Ella guessed that Zoltán Fazekas thought her not only lazy, but bone-idle into the bargain. It was beneath her dignity to tell him differently. 'Very commendable,' she murmured coldly, her chin tilting a proud fraction.

For long level moments, the cool grey eyes of the famous artist studied her, then, 'My apologies,' he offered aloofly. 'You were perhaps going to tell me that you keep house for your father?'

Ella gathered that her words 'My father...' and the fact that she knew one end of an iron from the other were responsible for that question. But she was proud again when, 'My mother runs our home superbly,' she replied, 'and, like you, we have a housekeeper.'

She looked at him, expecting him to have some blunt and to the point comment to make in answer, but realised that she was wasting her time thinking that she knew any of what was going on in his head when, having had sufficient to eat, apparently, he abruptly stood up.

'You will excuse me,' he requested courteously. 'I have an evening engagement.'

'Of course,' she answered proudly; she'd see him in hell before she'd remind him that she was his guest. 'Perhaps I'd better have an early night,' she murmured as he crossed to the door.

So much for sarcasm, she thought the moment he had gone. It hadn't even touched him, much less dented him. She had no need, though, to puzzle any longer on what it was he had against her, she realised. She knew then exactly what it was.

He knew, had more than likely concluded so from her father telling him that she would be available to sit for him at any time, that she was not one of the world's workers. It therefore followed that Zoltán Fazekas—who lived in a country where people had as many as four jobs—thought that she was nothing more than an idle layabout, and despised her for it.

Some while later, Ella climbed into bed, having, after much consideration, decided that she didn't care what he thought of her anyhow. Who was he to despise anybody, for that matter, leaving his guest to fend for herself on the first night in his home?

That since he'd never previously met her she couldn't be truly termed a guest, in the context of someone he wanted in his home, she acknowledged. But that still didn't excuse him.

Evening engagement, huh! she thought, and, feeling most decidedly disgruntled, she punched her pillow. It was quite obvious, of course, that there was some woman involved. Perhaps she, his woman friend, would be the one with mauve shadows from sleeplessness beneath her eyes come morning, Ella thought sourly.

Most oddly, though, as she lay down and closed her eyes, Ella felt quite disturbed. Somehow she didn't like at all the idea of Zoltán Fazekas and some other woman—how crazy!

CHAPTER THREE

EVERYTHING looked different in the morning. Ever an early riser, Ella got out of bed and straight away knew that she wasn't in the least disturbed, much less bothered, that Zoltán Fazekas had obviously had a heavy date last night. Good grief, he could have a hundred and one assignations, a hundred and one women friends, and it wouldn't bother her in the slightest. For heaven's sake, she'd only met him yesterday! And if he didn't like her, well, that went treble for her.

No, what really rankled, she reflected as she went and had her bath, was that he clearly thought her some lazy, frivolous female whose days were spent in one continuous round of pleasure. Far be it from her to tell him of her full days and long evenings spent as her indefatigable mother's first assistant and very often deputy.

Anticipating that no one would be abroad yet—for sure Zoltán Fazekas, if he was anything like David after a late night, wouldn't stir for another hour—Ella left her room and went lightly down the stairs. She was quite unconscious of the fact that her host was still as totally in her head that morning as he had been last night, as she made her way to the drawing-room.

She had her fingers on the handle of the drawing-room door, however, when, before she could turn it, Frida with a coffee-pot on a tray, appeared further up the hall from the direction of the kitchen.

'Jó reggelt,' the housekeeper greeted her.

'Jó reggelt,' she copied, and thought she must have got it right when Frida smiled. Though Ella had no idea

50

what she meant when, still pleasant-expressioned, she let go with a whole barrage of Hungarian. She found a clue, however, when after a moment, the housekeeper indicated the coffee-pot. 'Thank—er—*köszönöm*,' she amended, and, as Frida opened a door to a room Ella had not yet been in, so she went forward.

It was a breakfast-room, she saw as she entered. But so much for her being positive that Zoltán Fazekas would still be in his bed, dead to the world—he was there before her and already eating his breakfast.

'Good morning, Arabella,' he bade her urbanely, already on his feet, his eyes studying her face, her fine complexion, as he indicated that she take the seat opposite him.

'Good morning,' she replied, and took a chair at the breakfast table while Frida and her master exchanged a few comments.

'Frida wishes to know your preference for breakfast?' her host translated.

After two big meals yesterday, not to mention the roll and cheese she'd had for breakfast, Ella would have been happy with just a cup of coffee. But, with Frida being so pleasant, she had no wish at all to mess the woman about.

'I usually have just toast and marmalade at home,' she replied, sending a friendly look to his housekeeper as he conveyed the translation.

'*Tószt*,' Frida repeated, and, exchanging smiles with the houseguest, she went on her way.

'You slept well?' her host enquired.

'Like a baby—a good baby,' she qualified, and stared at him as though defying him to find any shadows under her eyes that morning.

She saw his mouth twitch as though her defiance amused him—but it could have been her imagination for there was no hint of a smile in his expression as he reached for the coffee-pot and poured her a cup.

'Thank you,' she murmured, but had other things on her mind. 'Mr Fazekas,' she began, 'can——?'

'Zoltán, please,' he cut in easily.

'Er—Zoltán,' she amended, oddly quite liking his name—and finding more than oddly, that she had forgotten what it was she wanted to say.

As she remembered though, Frida bustled into the breakfast-room with a small china rack of toast and a dish of marmalade—pats of butter were already there on the table—Ella delayed what she wanted to say for the moment. While she was in no hurry whatsoever to return to Thorneloe Hall—it went without saying, bearing in mind the nature of this latest upset, that hostilities at home were going to continue for some time yet—Ella was unused to enforced idleness and needed to be doing something, be it in this case only sitting. For sure, Zoltán Fazekas was going to start on her portrait today!

As soon as the housekeeper departed, Ella put her question. Though by then, bearing in mind that he'd definitely gone cool on her at dinner last night when she'd referred to it, she thought to wrap it up in a helping of tact, when, 'What sort of thing shall I change into?' she enquired as she reached for a slice of toast.

The silence emanating from opposite, caused her to raise her eyes to see what the artist made of her question. His cool assessing grey eyes were on her, she observed, and were taking in what he could see of the white shirt she had on and which was tucked into the waistband of a pair of tailored trousers.

His inspection of her over, however, 'You look perfectly respectable as you are, Arabella,' he drawled.

He was being deliberately obtuse, she felt sure but, with difficulty, she swallowed her ire. 'The others of the female Thorneloe line, were all painted in ballgowns,' she informed him as evenly as she could. 'I rather think that my father had that sort of thing in mind.' Her father was just going to love it, she thought, if, using an artist's prerogative, Zoltán Fazekas adamantly refused to paint her in anything but white shirt and trousers.

She was in fact warming to the idea of such a portrait hanging amid all the other bejewelled, silk- and satin-clad females when, 'You have a ballgown with you?' Zoltán enquired.

Her enthusiasm for the portrait, brief though it had been, abruptly faded. No shirt and trousers painting by the look of it! 'I didn't buy it specially to be painted in,' she answered tautly. 'I was supposed to be going to a ball tonight.'

He inclined his head to one side, 'The ball was cancelled?' he queried.

'No, I... that is...' She broke off. Damn him, why did she feel as though she had suddenly been wrong-footed? 'I decided to come here instead,' she told him woodenly—and brought yet more of his steady scrutiny.

'You're running away from something?' he enquired forthrightly.

'No, I'm not!' she vehemently denied.

'But you don't want your portrait painted?'

My stars, was he sharp! She could think of nothing that she'd said that could have given him that impression. Yet, he knew—he just *knew*! Oh, grief, she thought, fully aware that her father must have worked really hard to get an artist of such high calibre to agree to paint her. He would just about scalp her if she had to go home and confess that Zoltán Fazekas had refused the commission because she'd bluntly told him that she had no desire at all to have her likeness set down on canvas.

She raised her chin and was ready to lie to the Hungarian. But, strangely then, as she looked across at him, looked into those steady grey eyes that seemed to miss nothing, she found that the lie wouldn't come and that—she just couldn't lie to him.

'I...' She tried nevertheless, but had to amend what she'd been about to say to an honest, 'It's what my father wishes.'

Zoltán Fazekas continued to hold her gaze for a few seconds more then, idly almost, he leaned back in his chair, and then casually told her, 'Forget the ballgown— I'm not starting work on your portrait today.'

'You're not starting...' Annoyed, she broke off. While it was true that Hungary represented a nice safe bolt-hole at the moment, it went against the grain that she should kick her heels while she waited for him to feel the urge to make a start. 'I haven't got time to...' Her voice faded when she saw a glint of anger come to his eyes.

'What else have you in mind to do?' he rapped, his chin jutting aggressively, Zoltán Fazekas, a man of some tremendous talent, was clearly not impressed by her manner, she saw. 'From what you've said you've neither job nor urgent love-life to speed home for!'

'I have plenty——' She was angry too, and was in no mood to be flattened by this other tyrant who called her Arabella, though that was as far as she got, because he hadn't finished yet.

'You, with your life of petty detail, know nothing of the labours others have to perform!' he slated her.

Life of petty detail! If he only knew the sometimes back-breaking work she did! But clearly he was telling her that he'd got more important work to do that day than paint her. 'Well, bully for you!' she flew, her brilliantly blue eyes flashing sparks. 'Give me a ring when you can fit me in!' she hurled as she jumped to her feet.

'You're returning to England?' he was on his feet too.

'You ...' bet I'm returning, she'd been about to hotly state. But, she hesitated and oh, grief, she fumed impotently and, her temper cooling rapidly, talk about from the frying-pan into the fire!

'Your parents,' he took up, too smart to miss her hesitation, 'your father in particular, will be delighted to see you.' Was he taunting her? Was he daring to taunt ...? 'Delighted,' he continued, 'that you've taken flight from a duty which means so very much to him!'

'What do you mean?' she snapped.

'What would I mean?' he shrugged carelessly. 'You'll be twenty-two before this year is out, I believe.'

Ella started to get wary. Plainly this man knew of the background to do with this portrait. But, while she owned that it was natural that the artist would want to ask some questions of her father, in her view her father had told him much too much.

She tried a shrug of her own, 'So, I can come back before the year is out,' she answered offhandedly.

'True, you could,' he agreed, but added silkily, 'If I contacted you.'

Ella had never been certain that she had been going to light out anyway, but when it came to having one's bluff called she reckoned that she had just bumped up against an expert. 'You're saying that if I go now, my father can forget all about your having agreed to paint my portrait,' she stayed to challenge.

'I was right,' he drawled, and she could have sworn that there was a glint of humour in his look. 'You *are* an intelligent woman.'

'God spare me from temperamental artists!' she snorted and, having not been too bothered about breakfast anyway, she did a sharp about-turn and marched from the breakfast-room.

To show how much he cared whether or not she had breakfast, Ella was sure she heard the sound of his laugh follow her along the hall. Arrogant tyrant; far from cutting him with her remark about temperamental artists, she had actually amused the swine.

Half an hour later, having added a light sweater and a jacket to her shirt and trousers, Ella left the house. Apart from the fact that she was feeling too irked with Zoltán Fazekas to stay put, she decided that after two huge meals yesterday some exercise wouldn't come amiss.

Mutiny in her, though, was high as she stepped out on the pavements of the well-to-do area. It didn't take very much intelligence, however, for her to realise that Zoltán Fazekas with his artistic reputation, not to mention wealth, had no need whatsoever to paint her portrait. It was still a wonder to her that he'd agreed at all, but it was for certain, she acknowledged, that he would want her there, available, as soon as he'd finished the present work he was on. No way, he'd made that perfectly plain, was he going to hang around idly while she caught a flight back home—either she stayed put or she could forget about the portrait.

Strangely, then, especially when she considered that she'd never wanted her portrait painted to start with, she discovered that—she didn't want to go home. But what was most particularly strange about it was that she couldn't have said, in all honesty, that it was entirely on account of her father and the uproar of the moment concerning David. Nor, she faced with yet more honesty, did her aversion to leaving Hungary just then have any-thing to do with the fact that her father would, in addition to his wrath with David, create blue murder if she returned and scuppered any chance of Zoltán's painting her portrait after all the trouble her father must have been to.

Suddenly having become aware that Hungary must have woven some sort of spell over her while she wasn't looking, Ella decided that, since she was in no hurry to return to her temporary Hungarian home either, while she was out she would take a look at a very small part of the country.

All mutiny somehow faded when within the next two minutes she spotted a taxi approaching at speed. Even as the realisation sank in that if she didn't watch it she stood every chance of getting lost, she shot a hand out to flag him down.

She was sorry about the amount of tyre he left on the road as he screeched to a halt, but the taxi driver didn't seem to mind a bit as he beamed a smile at her and, she guessed, asked her where she wanted to be taken to.

'Er—can you take me to—er—your main square?' she asked him slowly, and crossed her fingers that he would be able to speak a little English.

To her gratification he did, even though he'd got her purpose slightly wrong, 'You want to see shops?' he enquired as she stepped into his taxi.

'No—er—monuments,' she plucked out of the air to correct him.

'Ah!' he acknowledged—and they were off. And, it seemed in no time at all, he was driving into a superb spacious area and telling her as he pulled over to let her out, '*Hosök tere*—Hero's Square. You want me wait?' he asked.

'No, that's all right, thank you,' Ella decided and with a courteous, '*Köszönöm*' she paid him, and for a long while admired the square with its august gateway to another area, before she walked towards it and to its most impressive monument, which had a central stone column that was topped with a statue of the Archangel Gabriel.

She was lost in admiration of the monument, her eyes roving to the base where seven magnificent equestrian statues were positioned, when she heard some nearby English-speaking tourist remark to a companion, 'That one must be Arpád with the six other vanquishing Magyar chiefs,' and at once Ella's thoughts flew to Zoltán Fazekas. These must be the same seven chiefs he'd spoken of last night when they'd dined on seven chiefs' *tokány*!

After that, as Ella sometimes walked, sometimes hopped in and out of taxis, it seemed that Zoltán Fazekas was forever in her head. For some unknown reason he stayed in her head while she browsed in a bookshop and, deciding that a sentence here and there in Hungarian might not come amiss, purchased a Hungarian phrasebook. She even at one point, as lunchtime hunger drove her into a restaurant, wished that Zoltán were there to guide her over the menu. Somehow she instinctively felt that he'd *know* that she'd chosen the wrong restaurant in which to sample her first dishful of Hungarian goulash. She was not totally impressed, but it filled a space and she felt less hollow when, on leaving the restaurant, she took yet another taxi.

Just because she did not want to have her portrait painted, it didn't mean that she could not appreciate art, so she was quite looking forward to a pleasant couple of hours when the taxi driver dropped her off at the Magyar Nemzeti Galéria. The Hungarian National Gallery occupied part of the former Royal Palace, and Ella took her time in wandering over the various floors that housed stone carvings, sculptures and paintings.

Paintings of portraits and landscapes but, disappointingly, none by the artist she was looking for.

Since, however, the paintings, so far as she could tell, only went up to 1945, she realised it was hardly surprising that Zoltán's work wasn't there—he hadn't been born then!

Ella glanced at her watch and, with astonishment, she saw that it was five o'clock! Grief—where had the day gone? It seemed a good idea to leave the gallery and to see if her luck held in the taxi-hailing department. It might be an idea too, since it had earlier worried her that she had slipped up badly in the manners section and had forgotten to tell Frida that she wouldn't be in to lunch—not that she'd been thinking of not returning when she'd left the house, it had just sort of happened—to put her phrasebook to use in finding some sort of apology.

Ella found a taxi without any problem and was soon speeding to her new and temporary home, and sitting back to realise that she had enjoyed her day immensely.

Frida opened the door to her ring, and Ella was swiftly dipping into her phrasebook, '*Bocsánat*, Frida,' she offered apologetically, and, when Frida just stared at her uncomprehendingly, '*Bocsánat, ebéd*,' she tacked on the word lunch.

'Ah,' Frida beamed, and offered a stream of smiling Hungarian which, from the accompanying smile, Ella took to mean a sort of 'think nothing of it'.

There was just time, she thought as she reached her room, for a short soak in the bath then, presuming *vacsora* was at eight again tonight, she'd better think about getting dressed for dinner.

Ella, dressed in a well-cut dress of pale lemon, was ready to go downstairs at seven-thirty. She had by then seriously considered the possibility that, since it was a

Saturday night, her host might have plans other than to keep her company over dinner. Not that after the short but angry exchange they'd had that morning she could expect him to take heed of the courtesies—she'd like to bet that it wasn't every day he discovered someone who didn't want her portrait painted by him.

Oddly, though, as she hesitated about leaving her room, she felt she would have quite liked to have told him about her day. A moment later, however, she was impatient with herself. Good grief, as if she cared! He was probably going out with the same female he'd had 'an engagement' with last night, she thought and, impatient with herself still, not to say irritated, she left her room.

You'd think, she thought five minutes later as she shared a pre-dinner drink with Zoltán in the drawing-room, that she'd never stirred him to anger! Never, conversely, made him laugh by calling him a temperamental artist. For, as though the way they'd flared up at each other at the breakfast table had never been, he was the most affable host.

Again Ella was struck by the whole being of the tall Hungarian in his well-cut lounge suit. She found, too, that she was quite happy to forget their spat—and also the fact that he had that morning laughed at her—when he remarked, 'I hear you've been out all day taking the air.'

Had he missed her, asked about her? Ella found she was wondering for some unfathomable reason. 'It was gone two o'clock before I realised that Frida might be expecting me back for lunch,' she felt drawn to reveal, and only then realised that he too might have expected to see her at the lunch table—clearly, her manners had gone to pot, 'I—er—felt dreadful about it. I should have...'

'From what Frida tells me, you apologised most prettily.' Zoltán made it all right again, and while Ella could not deny a flutter inside at his words, at the charm with which he said them, he was asking, 'Did you enjoy your day, Arabella?'

'Oh, so much!' she told him, her eyes shining. 'First I went to Hero's Square and, among other things, I saw the statues of the seven Magyar chiefs whom we were talking about only last night. Then I walked...'

Ella was still giving him a blow-by-blow account of her day when Frida came to tell them that dinner was ready. It was as she went with him to the dining-room, though, that Ella suddenly became appalled, and at once cringingly self-conscious. Oh heavens, she almost groaned out loud, what had come over her? Zoltán was sophisticated and then some—and here was she chattering on like some demented magpie! And about things—statues, monuments, museums—which he must know like the back of his hand anyway.

She drank her soup without so much as a peep escaping her. Though as she became aware that Zoltán had his glance on her, she hoped that she was either mistaken and that he wasn't glancing her way at all, or that if he was his artist's eye was assessing some feature or other. What she didn't want was that, after such a show of garrulity, he should be looking at her as though trying to work out why she should now be so silent.

She looked up, felt forced into it by *his* silence. But, while she was still feeling a bit of an idiot for having gone on so long, and that she could no longer be natural with him, quite evenly he enquired, 'The soup is too highly spiced for you?'

'It's delicious, thank you,' she replied coolly, observed from the one eyebrow that twitched aloft that he wasn't too enamoured of her tone and felt all at once anxious to show him that she wasn't so keen on his country as she might have sounded, and added, 'I thought I might take a trip into Austria tomorrow.' From having been determinedly silent for a few minutes, suddenly, at the much displeased look her host tossed her, Ella found she was babbling on again—this time about visiting the country on Hungary's western borders, something which, up until then, she hadn't given so much as a thought to doing. 'I could easily take a plane,' she suddenly felt swept along to continue, 'or a train for that matter.'

'Or even take the hydrofoil on the Danube to Vienna,' Zoltán cut in harshly. Then told her curtly, 'Clearly you believe that in a few hours you've seen all Budapest has to offer!'

She didn't think anything of the sort! Though, as she plainly saw that her host wasn't too thrilled about her stated plans for the next day, Ella realised that, by being over-sensitive, she had spoiled what had started out as quite a pleasant evening. On glancing at her harsh-expressioned host however, she was too proud to back down and suggest they start again.

The nearest she found she could go to capitulate, fairly loftily, she had to own, was to tell him in offhand tones, 'So I'll change my mind about Austria tomorrow, and go all touristy in Budapest instead. That is,' she tacked on quickly as the thought suddenly came to her, 'unless you're making a start on my portrait tomorrow.'

'Tomorrow,' he clipped, 'is Sunday!'

'Surprise me,' she muttered under her breath. 'You don't work Sundays?' she queried, feeling positive, no need to think about it, that when he was working there were no weekends and that all days would be the same to him.

He didn't lie and tell her that he didn't work Sundays, but she didn't thank him for that! Neither did she thank him for the grim, 'I'm not starting work on your portrait!' which he tossed at her icily—his very tone daring her to disagree.

At which point Ella decided it was beneath her to argue, and finished each course as Frida brought it without comment.

As soon as she could, and with a short and quiet 'Goodnight,' that went unanswered, and made her wish that she hadn't said a word, Ella returned to her room.

Swine of a man, she fumed, while she tried to sort out what in creation had happened to shatter her equilibrium since she'd arrived in this land. She hadn't felt so gawkish or awkward since her early teens, yet even then she couldn't remember ever having felt so thrown or so over-sensitive!

It was all his fault, of course, she decided, even if she wasn't at all sure what the fault was. With no intention of venturing down the stairs again that night anyhow, Ella went and got washed and changed into her night things to sit in a chair and pick up a paperback—which she never read.

Somehow, she felt between the devil and the deep. She felt niggled enough not to care that her father would create all hell if she arrived home with no portrait to follow—and with the message from Zoltán Fazekas that her return home meant that he was never going to paint her. And yet, at the same time, she still felt the most peculiar reluctance to leave!

CHAPTER FOUR

By MORNING, her equilibrium was fully restored, and Ella made her way down to breakfast of the opinion that the glass of *Badacsonyi kéknyelu* wine which she downed with her fish last night, had a lot to answer for. In truth, though, she had enjoyed the wine and, if memory served, she had been feeling more than a touch all over the place before she'd so much as taken a sip.

However, the sun was shining brightly that mid-September morning and, for all she knew that the sun would not have the strength of a full summer sun, it was a new day and if she enjoyed her sightseeing today half as much as she'd enjoyed it yesterday she would have no complaints.

Zoltán Fazekas was already at breakfast when she went into the breakfast room. She rather gathered that she would have to be up very early in the morning to beat him to it—and that went for everything else too.

But today she had established was a new day, and, '*Jó reggelt*' she greeted him as he courteously got to his feet. And, because of that new day, 'Zoltán,' she added, and took her place at the table.

'*Jó reggelt, Arabella*,' he replied suavely, and as he retook his seat, she decided that the all-fingers-and-thumbs, wishy-washy—not to say 'confused' creature she had been last night, was a person of the past. Time, she decided, to be positive.

'My friends call me Ella,' she told him pleasantly as with a more practised '*Köszönöm*,' she accepted from him the cup of coffee he had just poured for her.

64

What she had expected in reply, she was not at all sure. But what she definitely did *not* expect was that, artist that he was, Zoltán should look much deeper than the surface, and should come back with, 'You are not friends with your father?'

'Ah!' the exclamation escaped her half in surprise, half in acknowledgement that she should have realised that Zoltán was shrewd—and then some. Plainly, her father had only ever spoken of her to him as 'Arabella'. But, he was quietly waiting for an answer. 'Actually,' she felt compelled to go on, 'we—er—are very fond of each other, but...' she struggled—and then decided to give up searching for a way to explain how, love her father though she might, that didn't stop them from being bad friends for a good deal of the time '...but,' she resumed with an impish grin, 'my father finds me—er—very difficult to live with on occasions.'

She had her eyes fully on Zoltán, so was sure she would know it if he was thinking, I know exactly how your father feels. But she saw nothing of the sort, and began to realise then that she would most likely never be able to guess at what this man was thinking.

That realisation was indelibly underlined when, as she stared at him and he stared back, he suddenly declared, 'The astonishing blue of your eyes is, without question, most incredible,' and, while Ella was getting over her surprise at the unexpectedness of that comment, 'I prefer to call you Arabella,' he stated.

Ella took a sip of her coffee, and was quite foxed to know what to make of him. He had sounded quite friendly—well, as friendly as he ever would, she qualified. But, since she had only just told him that her friends called her Ella, was he, in some polite Hungarian way, telling her that he did not want to consider himself as one among her friends?

She had come to no conclusion other than that if Zoltán Fazekas wanted her to know something, it was unlikely, on what she knew of him so far, that he would wrap it up in politeness, when he suddenly startled her by saying, 'Your toast is keeping warm for you in this napkin,' and, as Ella got her wits together to realise that Sunday must be Frida's day off, 'Unfortunately, my housekeeper's rheumatism is plaguing her today,' he added.

'Frida suffers with rheumatism?' Ella questioned, recalling instantly how some of the elderly ladies she visited were afflicted with the same complaint, and aware of how exceedingly painful it could be. 'Oh, the poor dear!' she exclaimed before he could reply. And, ignoring that he looked startled at her sympathy for his housekeeper, 'Who laid the table for breakfast?' she asked him point-blank.

'Er—Frida,' he replied, and, looking a shade taken aback, 'You know something of rheumatism?'

'Some of my ladies endure agonies with it,' she answered.

'Your ladies?'

'I sometimes visit, make them a cup of tea...' Her voice faded as her thoughts centred on how Frida must have struggled to have done all she had that morning. 'I *do* wish you had given me a call, I——'

'A call?' he questioned mystified.

'I could have laid breakfast,' she explained, and went on when his attention seemed riveted on her, 'I could have seen to everything. Could——'

'Frida would not like that at all,' he cut in. 'She is a very proud woman, and insists on carrying on with her duties.'

'Oh, but we can't have that!' Ella protested, able-bodied and with energy to spare, while each movement must be agony for the woman who ran his house for him.

'Indeed, we cannot,' her host at once agreed, and sent her a smile of such warmth that, momentarily stunned by it, Ella forgot all about his incapacitated housekeeper. 'Which is why,' he went on, 'I've decided to take the day off. I,' he announced, 'will go touristing with you—if you wish it.'

'Yes... No... Well...' Ella stopped right there. She felt winded, knocked all of a heap. A moment later, however, she had recovered sufficiently to get her head together. 'You don't have to take me—er—touristing,' she began to protest. 'I'm quite capable of——'

'I'm sure you are,' he cut in pleasantly, 'but, even though I have instructed the good Frida that she must spend today resting, I fear that she will do nothing of the sort should I stay home. While I am here I'm certain she will believe she has to feed me.' He favoured Ella with another smile which, though not as heady as the previous one, nevertheless made her heart flutter again. 'Would you have me wander the streets of Budapest alone?' he enquired.

While Ella was positive that there were many doors in Budapest open to him—and she didn't have to look further back than his date of Friday evening to know of one—she found him just too much. His smile, what he had just said—without the charm that went with it, was much too much, and, as a smile tugged at the corners of her mouth, so laughter gurgled up inside her and she just had to burst out laughing.

For a moment or two Zoltán paused and just sat looking at her as though enjoying hearing her laughter, enjoying seeing her laugh. Then, as her laughter faded, 'Does that mean yes—that you'd like me to come with you?' he asked.

'I'd be delighted,' she replied, and was suddenly feeling all over the place again so reached for the napkin of toast, and concentrated her attention on that. Zoltán Fazekas, she was beginning to discover, could be far headier than any wine!

Ella did not lose sight totally of the plight of his housekeeper, however, and when not long afterwards she and Zoltán left the breakfast-room, she had a fair idea where Frida might be. If she was anything like Gwennie—who on one never-to-be-forgotten occasion when she'd been below par had had to be practically forced to go to her bed—then, regardless of how poorly Frida was feeling, she would be in the kitchen.

'You're a bit disorientated if you're intending to go to your room for an outdoor coat,' Zoltán reminded her casually when outside the breakfast-room door she turned right instead of left.

'I'll go up and get a jacket in a minute,' she replied lightly, and went on her way kitchenwards as she'd intended.

But her host was right there with her, she discovered as she reached down for the kitchen doorknob. His smile had gone into hiding, though, she observed, but she thought that he couldn't have any strong objections about her making free with his house, for he opened the door for her, and stood back to allow her to precede him.

'*Jó reggelt*, Frida,' she smiled, on seeing the house-keeper seated at a kitchen table reading what looked like a recipe book. 'Don't get up!' she exclaimed quickly as the housekeeper started to rise—and was heartily glad when over the top of her head Zoltán translated what she had just said into Hungarian.

At least Ella presumed he must have given Frida that or some similar instruction for with an answering, '*Jó reggelt,*' the housekeeper subsided back on to her chair.

Ella had her glance on the recipe book when it came to her that the housekeeper must be checking the details of something she intended to cook that day, and she made her mind up straight away. 'We can't possibly allow Frida to stand cooking for us today.' And, because in this situation Gwennie would have needed a lot of tactful handling, 'Do you think you could suggest that I'd love to try my hand in her kitchen and that I'd like to cook dinner tonight—and also that it would please me very much if she and Oszvald would be prepared to sample some of my English cooking?'

Ella was not sure that Zoltán did not do a double-take at her words. He most definitely looked startled at any rate as he enquired, 'You can cook?'

'Can't everybody?' she countered.

'You'd cook—for the four of us?' he asked amazed.

'At the risk of ruining my idle-layabout image—no problem,' she told him with a saucy grin, and as Zoltán addressed his housekeeper in his own tongue for some minutes, Ella felt quite light-headed at the prospect of being let loose in Frida's kitchen.

From then on the day took on a magical quality. Zoltán, she discovered, had more charm apart from that one glimpse she'd seen at breakfast, as he showed her things touristy, in Budapest.

Deciding against taking his car, he first of all took her by taxi to Adam Clark Square where they went and joined a small queue waiting for the *sikló*, the funicular railway. It was as they waited the few minutes for it to arrive that Zoltán gave her a brief history of the nearby Chain Bridge—one of the half dozen or so city bridges that spanned the Danube, the Chain Bridge noteworthy among other reasons because it was Budapest's first permanent stone bridge. An Englishman named William Tierney Clark had been commissioned to design the bridge and a Scottish engineer named Adam Clark arrived to supervise the work. The square at the Buda end was named after him and since in Hungary the family name always came before the first name the square was known as Clark Ádám tér.

The funicular ride did not take long and Ella could not deny a thrill of pleasure as she walked beside the tall Hungarian in the square of St George, and along cobbled streets.

'Since I've proclaimed this "Touristy Day" I've decided your education will not be complete without a visit to Matthias Church,' Zoltán informed her grandly, and Ella laughed, and was happy.

There had been a church on the site since before the thirteenth century but the present neo-Gothic structure of the Matthias Church was rebuilt just before the end of the nineteenth century, Ella learned, as she stood, walked, stood and gazed, at the church that had been one of the coronation churches of the kings of Hungary.

From there, they walked the Fishermen's Bastion, which was a series of stairways and open galleries and parapeted terraces in which Ella delighted and in true tourist style when recognised as a 'foreigner' was accosted by hardworking ladies, and shown any number of brightly embroidered traditional blouses. There were blue-embroidered tablecloths and white-embroidered ones to be seen too, along with other national crafts which Ella admired—all the while serenaded with music which came from a trio playing in the open air on instruments which were unknown to her.

The crowning moment for her, though, was as they walked around the area they crossed to view the dozens of small watercolours on display by various artists—students, she rather thought. One in particular caught her attention, a picture of a street-lamp and part of an amber wall, and not much else, but which she liked and, truly touristy, she decided to buy.

First, though, while managing to appear for all the world as though she'd forgotten her escort's mammoth reputation as an artist, she, wide-eyed, innocent and maybe just a little challenging, had to glance up at him. She was happier yet when, after some moments of solemnly staring down into what he had called the astonishing blue of her eyes, his expression fractured, and he all at once burst out laughing.

Her heart was tripping along merrily, however, when, as suddenly, his expression became serious. Her expression became serious too, though, when he insisted on paying for her picture.

'I *want* to pay!' she declared independently—but found that the deed was already done—the money having changed hands.

'Put it in your bag,' he decreed, passing it to her. And, when she opened her mouth to argue, 'You're hungry,' he decided, 'we'll eat.'

With some difficulty Ella swallowed down heated words that might have ruined what had been so memorable. Then, 'Yes, master,' she murmured sweetly, but saw his lips twitch just before he turned her about.

Any crossness that might have lingered at his highhandedness disappeared when, over a bowl of delicious-tasting soup, Ella discovered that Zoltán was a mine of information. He was never stuck for an answer, she found as, her interest in Hungary and things Hungarian for some reason suddenly avid, she plied him with questions.

In this way she learned that Hungarians had dwelt in the Carpathian basin for a thousand years or so. To the north-east of the basin was the high Carpathian mountain range, which arched in a semicircle from Czechoslovakia round to Romania.

'You were born in Hungary?' Ella found she'd left things impersonal to enquire as their soup dishes were exchanged for a plate of macaroni cheese that had smoked bacon in it, and which tasted gorgeous.

'Born here in Hungary, brought up here, and educated here,' he replied, and while Ella guessed that he must have been the star pupil in his art college or university she felt delighted that Zoltán seemed not a scrap offended that she had strayed into personal territory.

Most oddly, then, Ella discovered that her curiosity about him did not stop there! Indeed, her curiosity appeared to be suddenly insatiable as question after question sprang to her lips. She seemed quite unable to return to the subject of Hungary and its history just then, anyhow, as she asked, 'But you've travelled a tremendous amount, I believe?'

'I've visited one or two countries outside of my own,' he agreed, and Ella warmed to him—she had an idea that he'd been almost everywhere. She also liked the trace of a smile that lurked in his expression.

Encouraged, she found her inquisitive tongue was running away with her. 'Do your parents live here in Budapest too?' she enquired.

'They live in the western part of Hungary,' he answered easily. 'The climate's more humid there, but they like it.'

'Have——?' Suddenly she halted, and bit back the question she had been about to ask—had he any brothers or sisters? From the expression Zoltán wore he did not seem any more offended at her personal questions than he had been, but Ella was just starting to wonder where her curiosity would end. She'd be asking him about his aunts and uncles next!

'Have——?' he prompted—and Ella discovered that, in certain circumstances, she was able to pull off a lie of small consequence.

'I was just thinking that I've eaten so much that I don't think I'll have a pudding,' she replied—part of that statement was true anyhow; she didn't think she could eat another morsel.

To her relief Zoltán did not question what she said but, as though become aware that she was a woman with energy to burn, 'Care to walk?' he enquired.

'Please!' she accepted with alacrity, her expression alive and eager.

Zoltán did not move for a moment or two but just sat and looked at her, and gone was all trace of any cool aloofness which she had more than once seen in his eyes. Then, abruptly, he turned from her and called for the bill—and in next to no time they were striding up hill and down dale around Buda. Sometimes as they walked they would break into easy conversation on any subject that just seemed to crop up—but it was in the same amicable way that sometimes they walked along in silence.

The hour had just gone four when all at once Zoltán stopped, 'I nearly forgot—your English tea!' he declared, and, even while Ella laughed and protested that she could well do without it, he was guiding her to take tea—where somehow she also found room for a most delicious pastry.

It was almost six o'clock when Zoltán inserted his key into the door of his home and then stood back to allow her to go in first. Ella crossed in front of him, grateful to him for such a splendid time.

'I've had a super day!' she thanked him as they took a couple of paces into the hall.

'I'm glad,' he murmured, but somehow then as Zoltán looked down at her Ella experienced a sudden breathless feeling. Oddly, she was feeling all confused again—shy, almost.

Grief! she scorned. Shy! Nevertheless, she all at once experienced a need to be on her own, 'I'll—er—go and investigate in the kitchen,' she turned from him to state, recalling as she had occasionally through the day that she was cooking dinner that night.

Or so she had thought—until Zoltán touched a hand to her arm to prevent her from going kitchenwards, and, when she looked up at him enquiringly, 'I think we'd better eat out tonight,' he stated.

She looked away from him while her heart first of all raced that it seemed he wanted to take her out that night, then slowed down to a steady plod that he could equally well be saying that he had no appetite for English cooking. Confused, she realised, wasn't in it! Why should her heart race anyhow?

'Er—that sounds fine,' she replied as she suddenly became aware that he was waiting for some sort of comment. 'But—what about Frida and Oszvald's meal? Frida must——'

'Oszvald, believe me, is an excellent cook,' her host cut in, and from that moment Ella began to look forward to her evening out.

But, 'That's all right then,' she murmured composedly—only later in her room did she allow a smile to break free. She was going out with Zoltán tonight, and she was looking forward to it!

For some moments after that Ella tried to work out why the prospect of dining out with Zoltán Fazekas should make her feel so good inside. She couldn't remember ever feeling so—this way—before. Though she usually dined collectively with a small group of her friends. Or perhaps alone with either Jeremy Craven or Bertie Merriman, both of whom were men she'd known for donkey's ages, and neither of them, as nice as they were, what you could call particularly dynamic.

Ella went and had a shower and shampooed her hair, to return from the bathroom having accepted that it must be Zoltán's dynamism that was responsible for the flurry in her excitement department.

Having satisfactorily dealt with that, she went over to the wardrobe wondering what she should wear. Should she dress up, or down? Where would Zoltán take her? She did so wish that she'd thought to ask.

In the end it was impatience with herself, for she could never remember being so indecisive about what to wear before either, that saw her opt for a fairly new dress of deep green velvet that particularly suited her. Its neckline was cut low and showed off her smooth pale skin to perfection. Ella finished off the ensemble with her last birthday present from her parents, a double strand of pearls.

For no reason she could think of, she realised that she was feeling a little nervous when, with her newly washed hair about her shoulders, she was ready to leave her room. Then she glanced down at her dressing-table and her eyes lit on the small picture she had taken from her bag, and which he had purchased that day. Suddenly then, as she remembered how good that day had been, how superb a companion Zoltán had been, so her confidence all at once returned. With a smile curving her lovely mouth, she picked up her evening purse, and went toward her bedroom door.

She was halfway down the elegant staircase when Zoltán suddenly appeared in the hall, looked up, and abruptly halted. Momentarily, as her heart suddenly picked up its beat, Ella halted too. A second later, she went down the stairs to join him.

'May I state the obvious? You're beautiful,' he said solemnly, when as they stood together in the hall he looked down at her.

Ella tried hard for a trite, 'You may, any time,' but the words got stuck in her throat, and all that came out, was a husky, 'Thank you.'

Zoltán took her to one of Hungary's most famous restaurants, Gundel's. It was situated in the City Park, just off Hero's Square where she'd been yesterday morning. A doorman was there to see them into an ante-room where to the left was a settee and chairs in matching mustard-coloured velvet, and to the right was the cloak check area. Though barely had they entered when the head waiter came and escorted them through to an inner sanctum.

The evening, that had for some unknown reason had something 'special' about it from the start, became somehow enchanting. She rather thought that the man seated opposite might have something to do with it, for, having already thought of him as quite something of a real man, in a dinner-jacket, Ella realised, he was that, *plus*!

She was barely aware of what she ate, but while a sextet of musicians played gypsy music in the background she had a growing awareness of Zoltán Fazekas. He could, all too easily, prove far more potent than the Hungarian Pinot Noir they were drinking, she realised— if she allowed him to be.

Which was totally ridiculous, she fully owned a moment later, because, for her to 'allow' anything, Zoltán would first have to state, or show, some sign that he saw her as anything but some female whom he was forced to put up with for a while.

She couldn't read anything into the fact that he had brought her out to dine, because, with Frida incapacitated, to him it would seem an obvious thing to do. Nor did the fact that he thought her beautiful mean anything more than that, as an artist, he admired her bone-structure.

More haunting gypsy music floated across and was no help whatsoever in Ella's quest to get herself on a more even keel. Just then however, an attentive waiter came and topped up her glass and after a whispered, '*Köszönöm*,' Ella made great efforts to take her mind off Zoltán by concentrating her attention on the flowers on the table, on the pink velvet of the chairs, on the discreet lighting—on anything. Then suddenly Zoltán made some comment, and she was overwhelmingly aware of him again.

'So,' he remarked conversationally, 'you're not running away from anything?' She turned her head to glance at him, but as she looked into warm grey eyes she was lost to know what he was talking about. A second later, however, some part of her normally bright and alert brain woke up to give her a nudge.

'Oh—I thought you'd forgotten that,' she smiled, realising at the same time that this breathtaking man forgot nothing—and that included a conversation that they'd had at breakfast-time yesterday.

He smiled, in return, but insisted, 'So?' and Ella knew then that he wanted to know why she had come to have her portrait painted when she was so against it.

'Er...' she delayed, and there on the end of the tongue was a question she had wanted to ask him at lunchtime. 'Have you any brothers or sisters?' she enquired, and gave him full marks that he did not so much as blink at the unexpectedness of her question.

'No,' he replied, but his eyes were watchful.

'Then you may not know that—sometimes—when one's sibling gets into hot water—in this case, my brother,' she found she was telling him openly, 'it seems politic to—er—take off for a while until the yelling stops.'

For some moments Zoltán silently studied her then, clearly having worked out a lot of it, 'Your parents are angry with your brother over some matter which had repercussions for you?' he questioned.

'My father,' she corrected. 'My mother's an absolute angel.'

'I see,' Zoltán replied, and, with his eyes fixed on hers, as if daring her to lie, 'So, had your brother not got into "hot water",' he resumed, 'you would not have come to Hungary at all?'

For a moment Ella was stumped, then, 'Are you going to blame my brother for that too?' she asked. 'My turning up here, I mean?' she added with a sudden smile. But when to her delight a smile tugged at the corner of Zoltán's mouth too, and her heart, she would swear, turned a crazy somersault, Ella found she had a quite desperate need to add something else. 'Actually,' she impulsively confessed, 'I'd have come anyway. I—er—just need a little more—er—pushing.'

'You have stubbornness,' he stated rather than asked.

'No!' she replied at once, but, as his right eyebrow quirked most fascinatingly aloft, 'Well, I might just... Can we change the subject?'

His answer was to raise his glass, 'Welcome to Hungary, Arabella,' he saluted her.

By the time they left Gundel's and a taxi had dropped them off at Zoltán's home, Ella was feeling quite euphoric. Indeed, she had enjoyed her evening so much that she could not remember when, if ever, she had kicked against coming to Hungary.

She waited in the hall while Zoltán bolted the front door after them, but as they walked towards the stairs she unexpectedly felt that she wanted to tell him that she liked his country and that she wished that she had come sooner.

They were passing by the open drawing-room door when abruptly she halted and in the same suddenness, turned swiftly—and cannoned into him. Then, whatever she had been going to say to him—if anything at all— went straight from her head, because as Zoltán shot out a hand as if to save her from falling, so his other arm came around her—and as she looked at him, so she was lost.

How they came to be so warmly embracing she neither knew nor cared. All she was aware of was that as his arms were around her, so her arms were around him. Then, as he gently gazed into her wide blue eyes, so his head started to come down, and... their lips met.

Ella had been kissed before, but never like this! There was no mistaking his expertise as Zoltán held her close up against him and with his mouth over hers drew the very soul from her. Then, while she was clutching at him for support, his mouth left hers and he placed whispers of kisses down the side of her face, down the arched column of her throat, and down the silky smooth skin to the low neck of her dress.

Quite when they moved from the hall into the drawing-room Ella never knew. But Zoltán's lips were on hers again when she surfaced a little way to realise that they were half sitting, half lying in the deep comfortable cushions of a plumply stuffed couch—and that one of Zoltán's hands had just gently caressed to capture her left breast.

'I—er...' she murmured, and, feeling dizzy at the emotions he had awakened in her, she moved, while she still could, to break his hold.

Immediately Zoltán removed his hand from her breast—and immediately Ella wanted his hand back where it had been again. Oh, help me somebody, she thought, and as another moment of strength arrived she grabbed at it, and stood up.

But she felt weak again when Zoltán, on his feet too, his expression pensive, looked down at her and, 'What—er—sort of a girl do you think I am?' she found a smile to joke. She did not want to part bad friends but knew that her bedroom was safer than the drawing-room just now, and that she ought to get there with all speed.

For a while, a brief while, she thought that they were going to part as enemies, for, from looking pensive, Zoltán had gone to look more than a little taken aback—not to say stunned.

But, when Ella was mentally bracing herself for trouble if he had read more encouragement from their exchanged kisses than she'd realised and was not prepared to take 'no' for an answer, she was the one to be taken aback. For, 'You—have—been kissed before?' was the question which he put to her sternly. And she realised yet again that she would never comprehend what went on behind that clever forehead.

Quickly, though, she recovered, and answered his question in the only honest way that she could.

'I—er—used to think so,' she told him, and, when he just stood and stared down at her in that stunned kind of way for more long long moments, she did the only thing possible—she grinned up at him.

And it was then, that he took a step back from her, and formally decreed, 'I think, Miss Arabella Thorneloe, that you had better go to your bed.'

There were many things with which she wanted to reply. She wanted to thank him for her lovely evening, wanted to thank him for his understanding, for his unspoken acknowledgement that her room was the safest place for her just then. But, above all, she just then discovered, she wanted him to kiss her again—just once.

But, if he did kiss her again, it wouldn't stop at one kiss—she would want more, she knew as she glanced to his wonderful mouth that she would. Just as she knew, sensed, that, while Zoltán was a man of some self-control, his self-control was at a very low ebb at this moment.

'Goodnight,' she bade him quickly, on a breathless sound, and while she still could she went smartly from the room—gypsy music, she decided, had a lot to answer for.

CHAPTER FIVE

ELLA was awake long before dawn the following morning. Though throughout the night she had lived and relived the headiness of Zoltán's kisses. Had that really been Zoltán who had last night turned her knees to water? Had that electrifying man really been the same cool-eyed man whom she'd met but a few short days ago? More intriguing than that, though, had that really been *her*?

By the time Ella decided it was time to desert her bed and to get on with her day she had wondered for so long about the new and emotionally haywire person whom Zoltán with a few ardent kisses and caresses had brought to the surface that her head was spinning again. Quite clearly there were hidden depths of passion in her which she had never known about—but which Zoltán...

But enough was enough. She got out of bed resolving to put such thoughts, such nonsense behind her. Today was another day—she would get bathed and dressed and then, in the same way in which she and her mother lent a hand when Gwennie or any of the other staff were under the weather, she would go and help Frida.

Having decided that she had been idle for long enough, Ella left her room and descended the stairs, trying to ignore that her insides seemed all of a flutter at the thought of seeing Zoltán again.

As she had anticipated, he was already at breakfast when she entered the breakfast room. But although she had planned for the past half-hour to be pleasant, even-toned, and to act as if nothing out of the ordinary had taken place between them, she was straight away thrown completely off balance. First of all because a maid she hadn't met before was placing a coffee-pot upon the table, but much more particularly because as she flicked a glance at Zoltán she met his level-eyed look full on, and she was quite unprepared for the riot of emotion that stormed her. It was that unexpected riot of emotion which unfortunately caused her 'Good morning,' to come out sounding sharp and staccato—unfriendly, even—but in no way at all as pleasant and as level as she had planned.

Swiftly she subsided into her usual seat and was reaching for her serviette when, 'Good morning, Arabella,' Zoltán answered her greeting crisply. And not forgetting his duties as host, 'You slept well?' he enquired.

Was he being funny? After his kisses! After the tumult of emotion he'd awakened in her—the hours of self-analysis he'd instigated? Not to mention just *him*! But, 'Exceptionally well,' she replied stiffly, and, that conversation closed as far as she was concerned, she glanced at the maid who seemed about to leave, 'Is Frida no better this morning?' she asked.

'This is Nadja,' Zoltán introduced the maid, and as Ella exchanged a smile with her and the maid went on her way, 'Nadja has had a long weekend off, but has been with us some while,' he added coolly.

Which was one polite way of saying that he had enough staff to cope if one of them went down ill, Ella thought, sensitive enough at that moment to feel irked by what, in her sensitive state, she saw as a snub. She accepted the cup of coffee he poured and handed to her with a taut, 'Thank you,' but then found that she had too much about her to be sat upon by anyone, and that included him. So, uncaring whether she was being over-sensitive

and that he might not have intended to snub her offer
of help before she could make it, 'Once I've had
breakfast, I'll go along and give Frida a hand,' she announced, a trace defiantly she had to own—so wasn't
totally surprised when Zoltán paused to study her coolly
for some moments, in a way she was getting quite used
to.

She knew he wasn't enamoured with her offer, though,
and that was before, 'That won't be necessary!' he
clipped.

Clearly the man had no idea of how painful rheumatism was! 'Frida should be resting and not——'

'Thank you for your concern,' he chopped her off,
then told her cuttingly, 'Frida is better this morning and
would be offended should you wish to take over her
duties.'

'I don't want to take over!' she erupted angrily,
sending him a dagger's look, and knowing then that she'd
cut her tongue out before she'd make a similar offer.
But feeling incensed all at once, 'What, if I'm not allowed to help out, do you suggest I do all day?' she
demanded—and for her sins was made to suffer another
of his cold, and suddenly arrogant looks.

'Do I assume that you are always busy with something?' enquired he who knew full well that she had no
paid job.

Sarcastic swine, she fumed, but as Nadja came in with
a rack of hot toast Ella was suddenly taken with the
appalling thought that maybe Zoltán thought she had
been hinting that he should take the day off and take
her around sightseeing.

'*Köszönöm, Nadja,*' she smiled, while inwardly she
died a thousand deaths as she wondered how to convey
to her host that she'd cut off her toes sooner than tramp
the pavements of Budapest with him again.

But with nothing brilliant coming to her she took the opportunity to glare at him as she helped herself to a slice of toast. For some reason, however, her glance strayed to his mouth and suddenly as she remembered the feel of that well-shaped mouth over hers so her anger disappeared. Indeed, she felt so weakened by the memory when, clearly, he hadn't given another thought to the kisses they'd shared—or if he had, only to regret them—that she found she was having to fight hard to hide it.

She reckoned, though, that she had managed it superbly when, her tone more belligerent than weak, she enquired shortly, 'Are you going to make a start on my portrait today?'

His answer was to look at her long and hard. But, when she fully expected to be on the receiving end of something short and pithy for a reply, to her surprise he chose not to assault her ears with a few well-chosen words for her sauce, or for that matter to reply to her question at all, but informed her, coolly, it was true, 'Today, I have decided, we will move to my other home.'

'Other home?' she enquired, shaken enough to forget to be angry. 'Where . . . ?'

'It's on the shores of Lake Balaton—about a couple of hours' drive from here.'

'I . . . W . . .' Staring at him, somewhat stunned, Ella strove to get her head together. 'W-we're all going?' she managed to get out at last.

'Nadja will stay here,' he replied, then abruptly he stood up, and, his tone the bossiest yet, she thought, he ordered, 'Be ready in an hour!'

'Certainly, Colonel!' she flew. Though, when without another word he strode to the door, she had the oddest notion that she had spotted a grin doing its best to tug up the corners of his mouth. She hoped not. It would be just too much if she had amused him again.

There was no sign, however, that he was in any way amused when an hour and a quarter later she stood with him in the hall while he gave her cases a baleful glance.

'Did you leave *anything* at home?' he enquired sarcastically, and she quite hated him. But, unable to find anything cutting enough by way of reply just then, she favoured him with an arrogant look of her own, and then reached down for one of her cases—and found that that wasn't right either when he barked, 'Leave that!'

Ella straightened but, when it was still on the cards that she would defy him and manhandle her own luggage, Oszvald suddenly appeared from nowhere, and while he claimed one of her large suitcases Zoltán carried the other out to his car.

'Are Frida and Oszvald not travelling with us?' she enquired when soon afterwards she was seated beside her host, and he set his car in motion.

'They will follow later,' he replied shortly, and that was about the extent of their conversation.

Ella owned to feeling a shade peeved with him and his attitude as they drove on and left Budapest behind. Nor did she wish to feel any differently. He was, she decided, a most confusing man. But, when in silence they had driven for over an hour, so again and again her eyes were drawn to his hands on the steering wheel. They were agreeable-looking hands, she contemplated, long-fingered, sensitive, artistic.

A touch of whimsy smote her and she fell to wondering how such a man as he could have such sensitive-looking hands when she knew him to be such a sharp-tongued brute.

Not many minutes later, though, an innate fairness had surfaced in Ella, and she was delving into the territory of—what had she expected? Her greeting to him that morning had hardly been filled with sweetness and light. How was he supposed to have reacted to *her* sharp tone, for goodness' sake? Was he supposed to have said something along the lines of, 'I take it you didn't like my kisses?' His kisses—oh, heavens, she'd been completely mindless from the moment his lips had touched hers. So much for not liking his mouth on hers; lord knew where it would have ended had not she recovered a moment's sense when his hand had captured her breast.

'Do you often come to your other home?' she asked in a sudden rush to get away from her thoughts.

'We're here!' he announced tersely, hostilities apparently still on, and Ella wished that she'd kept her mouth shut.

Even while her mind had been fully occupied with her thoughts, Ella had nevertheless been aware of the changing countryside around her. They were in an area where town and city were far behind, and were passing by a screen of tall poplar trees, when Zoltán turned the car and drove up a long winding drive to a stately-looking stone-built house at the top.

In view of his terse 'we're here!' of a few minutes earlier, however, Ella swallowed down any comment and moved from the car and on to the gravelled drive, and then went with her host up the stone steps to his house.

No sooner had they stepped inside the hall, though, than a pretty overall-clad woman of about thirty appeared, and, 'Ah, Lenke,' Zoltán addressed her, and conversed with the woman for a minute or so, then, turning to Ella, he suggested, 'If you would like to go with Lenke, she will show you to your room.'

'Thank you,' Ella murmured politely, and as he went off in one direction she and the maid went off in another.

By the time Lenke had shown her up the stairs to what was another very comfortably appointed bedroom with its own bathroom, Ella guessed it was established that she didn't speak Hungarian. Though she thanked her in Hungarian and received a lovely smile before the maid went off about her other duties.

Thinking to go downstairs shortly and, if allowed, collect her luggage, Ella went over to one of the two large windows in her room and looked out to discover that she had a simply superb view of part of the massive Lake Balaton. As the front of the house was well screened by poplars, so too was the rear of the building by many trees and much vegetation, but in no way did nature's natural concealment impede her view.

With the idea in mind to do a little exploring at some date, Ella turned from the window on hearing someone rap on her door. 'Oh—er—thank you!' she exclaimed on seeing Zoltán had beaten her to it and had brought up her cases.

He did not at first have any comment to make, but stood looking down, surveying her from his lofty height, though as his glance slid down to her slightly parted lips he turned abruptly about. 'Lunch will be at two!' he grunted over his shoulder, and was gone.

Ella spent what time remained until a quarter to two in unpacking a few of her things, getting washed and changed into a classically cut day-dress, and then, having wondered what on earth was the matter with her in that what she had been wearing before had been quite all right to lunch in, she changed back again.

At five to two, she left her room and went down the stairs to see that Frida had arrived. '*Jó napot*,' she greeted the housekeeper cheerfully, pleased to see her as the other beamed a smile at her and answered her greeting, and then showed her to the dining-room.

Ella was feeling much less cheerful a half an hour later when, her meal almost finished, she had seen no sign of her host. She finished her main course, feeling glad suddenly that she had not changed for lunch after all. Not that she'd changed in the first place for Zoltán Fazekas's benefit, she very quickly decided.

She felt quite annoyed with herself, however, when, absolutely certain that she didn't give a hoot where her host was, she heard herself asking Frida, 'Er— Fazekas *ur*...?' Having said 'Mr Fazekas...' she left the question open-ended, and was most grateful when Frida quickly caught on.

Though as the housekeeper let go with a flurry of Hungarian there was only one word in all of it that made any sense to Ella, and that word was 'studio'.

'*Köszönöm*, Frida,' she smiled, and realised that of course, in the same way that he had a studio in his Budapest home, Zoltán had one here too. Her host, she realised, must obviously have felt some burning need to get down to work straight away.

Ella was back in her room busy with the rest of her unpacking when she suddenly started to feel quite niggled. She didn't mind a bit that Zoltán felt the artistic urge to do some painting, to do some work, but it wasn't work on her portrait, was it?

She tried hard not to get cross that she was left awaiting *his* pleasure, but owned that she found it difficult. True, he was a great artist, and she couldn't and shouldn't expect him to drop everything just because she'd arrived. And true, she hadn't anything too pressing which she should be doing, she had to admit. But, as she did her best to bury her ire, Ella sighed that things generally just didn't seem to be working out very well lately.

When she had hung the last remaining item from her case on a hanger, Ella saw from the overcast sky that perhaps, with evening fast approaching, she had left it too late to go exploring as she had half intended. From what she could tell, Zoltán did not appear to have any near neighbours, so it did seem a little foolhardy to go investigating anywhere. She had an idea that, with darkness about to descend, Zoltán would just love it if she got lost and he had to come looking for her.

Ella dressed for dinner in a pale green dress of fine jersey wool. I won't be cross, I'll be pleasant and friendly, she decided, as she went slowly down the wide staircase at a few minutes before eight. And, while being pleasant and friendly, she would, at some time during dinner—always supposing Zoltán wasn't short and sharp and didn't stir her to retaliate in kind—ask him, politely, if he could give her some idea of when he was going to start work with her. Always supposing too, of course, that he was there at the meal table tonight.

'Good evening, Arabella!'

Strangely, she felt her heart lift when, just as she reached the bottom tread, her host came out from one of the rooms across the hall. 'Good evening, Zoltán,' she answered pleasantly, adding Zoltán at the end as the friendly bit.

'Care for a drink?' he enquired, strolling the step or two to the next-door room and holding the door open for her.

'A small one,' she smiled, and went into what turned out to be a drawing-room.

While Zoltán went over to a drinks table and busied himself with the small gin and tonic she normally favoured, she looked about at the deep-piled plain carpet and the pair of patterned three-seater settees in the room, and other comfortable-looking chairs.

'You've been busy working this afternoon, I believe,' she thought to mention as a warm-up to what she had to ask him when he came back and handed her her drink.

'What have you been doing?' he enquired, which took the conversation entirely away from where she wanted it.

'Unpacking. I...' She was about to try to get the conversation back to where she wanted it when, most unexpectedly, his mouth began to curve in good humour and, looking at his mouth, what she was going to say went from her.

'But not ironing, I trust?' he enquired, his tones teasing.

'I—er...' she began, but as her heart did a silly little giddy leap at his pleasantness she decided, all else escaping her, that she'd better pretend to take him literally. 'My clothes—travelled better this time,' she replied, but, as her eyes rested on his pleasantly curving mouth, so she just couldn't hope to prevent a matching curve coming to hers.

His glance flicked over her face and then stilled, but she realised it was just the artist in him that caused his glance to rest on her, to stay on her. When his glance seemed suddenly to grow warmer, Ella discovered that she was feeling quite breathless—and quite confused when he opened his mouth to suggest, 'Frida will have taken the soup to the dining-room—shall we take our drinks through?'

Strangely, from that moment on, Ella started to feel oddly restless. Even as she went with him to the room which she remembered from lunchtime, she felt edgy, unable to settle.

Frida had served the first course when Ella determined that her feeling of restlessness could only stem from the fact that she wanted a straight answer to a straight question. That being so, she endeavoured to lose her feeling of restlessness without delay—there seemed no time like the present.

'I wonder,' she spoke up clearly as she placed her soup spoon down, 'if you can give me any idea—Zoltán,' again she added his name so he should know that she wasn't trying to demand—something that didn't seem to go down too well she'd discovered—but was being friendly, 'when you intend to work on my portrait?'

His answer was to lay down his soup spoon too, but only so that he could very deliberately study her. Then, his expression totally serious, 'You must not be impatient, Arabella,' he instructed, his tone even. 'You must give me time.'

'Time?' she enquired, with his intense gaze full on her, suddenly starting to feel all anyhow. 'What—er—sort of time?' she asked, but even as she was wondering if he meant that she should go away and return when it was more convenient—though he'd objected to that sort of an idea before—he was letting her know that he wanted her nowhere but where she was.

'You must allow me time to know my subject,' he enlightened her, and Ella wasn't at all sure how she felt about that. She quite realised that a part of how he came to produce such wonderful work—which had earned him worldwide renown—was through his searching with his artist's eyes right to the heart of his subject. But the fact that he intended to search, to delve deeper, so that he could put the 'real' her down on canvas, made her feel defenceless somehow.

'Er—me, you mean?' she queried slowly, aware that she was playing for time.

His mouth curved upwards. 'Who else?' he enquired.

Ella moistened her top lip with the tip of her tongue, a nervous gesture. 'How long will that take, do you suppose?' she asked, and felt suddenly all of a fluster when that upward curve became a definite smile.

'A lifetime, I shouldn't wonder,' he replied, and there was such charm in him all at once that from that moment Ella started to feel unexpectedly better about everything.

'I don't think I can spare you that long,' she murmured, her expression serious, but laughter lurking there in the wide blue eyes which she turned to him.

'Then I shall have to hurry up,' he stated pleasantly, his eyes fixed on hers. But, when from what he had just said she had formed the notion that he would start work on her portrait tomorrow, he surprised her by saying nothing remotely similar, but, 'I know of your brother and his penchant for getting into hot water,' he began, 'and I have met your father, so,' he paused, then, looking steadily at her, continued, 'so tell me, Arabella, about your mother.'

'My mother!' she exclaimed startled.

'You didn't get your incredible colouring from your father,' he smiled.

Oh, my word, this man was something else again! Ella felt as if her brain had gone on holiday as she coped with what she thought was a compliment—he had a smile that would melt the hardest heart!

'Er—actually, my mother's colouring is quite different from mine,' she got herself together to reply. 'Though I rather think I'm a bit of a throw-back from her side of the family. There's not a redhead on the staircase, anyhow,' she revealed, then abruptly halted, aware that she was gabbling.

But, 'The staircase?' he encouraged.

'The portraits of the twenty-one-year-old Thorneloe women,' Ella explained. 'We've got a whole staircase full of them.'

'But so far not one redhead?'

'Not one,' she replied, and suddenly wanted the conversation away from herself. 'But you were asking about my mother,' she quickly changed the subject. 'Now there's a fantastic lady if you like.' Ella started to feel better again, and because she quite enjoyed talking of her parent she launched into an account of how her mother was on this committee and that, and included the information that, while her mother was chairperson of another group, she was also a school governor as well as a hospital visitor. In short, with her face alive with interest and affection, she revealed how tireless her mother was if anyone needed help—and could have gone on *ad infinitum*. But, since Zoltán had never met her mother, even if he had asked about her, Ella settled for giving him a few instances of her mother's selflessness in assistance to others, and looked up to smile, 'So you see, I wasn't exaggerating when I said that she is one fantastic lady.'

And got the shock of her life when, with another of his level looks, Zoltán murmured quietly, 'And you, I'm beginning to think, are set in a very similar mould.'

'Me!' she exclaimed, astonished. 'How do you make that out?'

He shrugged, but replied pleasantly, 'You were so carried away when telling me of the time your mother, with some helpers, made a duck supper for the local old people's club she oversees that you were entirely unaware of the times you said "we". I very much suspect, little Arabella, that you are thoroughly involved in not one but very many of her activities. Indeed,' he went on while Ella was feeling quite intoxicated just from those two words 'little Arabella', 'it is no wonder to me that *you* have no paid occupation. As your mother's first lieutenant, when would you find the time?'

'Er—yes—well,' Ella mumbled, but again felt awkward at having the conversation brought round to her once more, so smiled as she brightly confided,

'Anyhow my mother's having a jolly good rest now,' and going quickly on, 'She's on holiday in——' As swiftly as she had started, so her voice abruptly ended.

'Her holiday destination is a secret?' Zoltán prompted at once, as sharp as a tack, she realised.

But she shook her head. 'No, not exactly,' she replied, and, while she had no intention of saying anything further on the matter, she discovered, to her absolute astonishment that, at the encouraging look he showed her, she was actually going on to reveal, 'With my father being so irate at my brother's—er—at the moment, I sort of thought it better that my mother should enjoy her holiday without... That is...' She faltered.

'Your father doesn't know where she is?' Zoltán astutely questioned, and Ella felt it sounded quite terrible.

'He knows that she's in South America,' she said hurriedly, but, at Zoltán's steady look, felt forced to add, 'But—er—not exactly where.'

'And you've taken pains—before you left England—to see that he doesn't find out?' her host, astute not the word for it, suggested.

'I...' she began, and suddenly felt dreadful. How she had come to say as much as she had she had no idea, but all at once she was starting to feel overwhelmingly disloyal. 'I expect my father knows by now, anyhow,' she commented, and, hoping that Zoltán would see that she wanted this conversation ended, 'My mother's bound to have rung home by now.'

'I'm sure she has,' he replied suavely, and centred the conversation away from England, and, as she wanted, away from anything to do with family.

When later that evening Ella climbed into bed, though, she was still wondering what it was about the man that had seen her revealing that which normally wild horses wouldn't have seen her revealing—particularly to a man like him! For it went without saying that a man with his gift for seeing through to the heart of things would have soon pieced together, from the few snippets she had given him, that her home-life was not always all that harmonious.

Ella turned over in her bed, realising that Zoltán would have known that before this evening anyway. She had left him in no doubt that she wouldn't be here now but for her brother being the cause of a rumpus.

She turned over again and decided to concentrate on other things. For one, now when the dickens was Zoltán going to start painting her picture?

CHAPTER SIX

A WEEK later, Ella was upstairs in her room running a tidying comb through her hair prior to going down to lunch, and was still wondering when in creation Zoltán was going to start work on her portrait.

Life at his Lake Balaton home had fallen into some sort of routine where, although she saw her host every morning at breakfast, she sometimes did not see him again until dinner in the evening. Ample time on both occasions, she knew, in which she could ask him again about when he intended to start work. But in her view she had asked him enough times; she was jolly certain she would not ask him again.

She placed her comb down on the dressing-table and reflected how some time around last Tuesday she had made up her mind that on the occasions when she was in his company she would have little to say to him. Perhaps then, she'd thought, he would get fed up with having her monosyllabic person around and would get started on her portrait 'the sooner to finish'. But, for all her determination not to enter into any sort of conversation with the man, somehow, and she still wasn't certain how, he always managed to disarm her.

Was it the charm of the man? she wondered. Was it the fact that he was mostly affable towards her these days that was responsible for her forgetting what she'd determined upon? Seen her forgetting and responding to a question, so that soon they were deep in conversation anyway. Or perhaps it was just her upbringing, the basic good manners instilled in her from childhood which, although having suffered a hiccup or two when she'd first arrived, had settled down to remind her that, whatever else, she was still a guest in his home.

But, Ella thought, the light of battle in her eyes, she'd had enough, more than enough. It seemed to her then as she tripped lightly down the stairs that after a week of waiting it was time she changed her tactics. Clearly, not to ask him again when he was going to start work on her picture, had been wrong.

She crossed the hall to the dining-room considering that the only other option she had was of asking him at every mealtime when he was going to make a start. Maybe if she made him fed up enough he'd show her to his studio just to shut her up.

Her decision made, Ella opened the dining-room door hoping with all she had that this wouldn't be one of those lunchtimes which Zoltán chose to work through. The flutter in her insides when she saw that she was to have his company for lunch because he was already there stemmed, she knew, only from the fact that, having just spent a week without so much as a cross word passing between them, it was on the cards that that state of affairs wasn't going to last. Not when she demanded to know when she should present herself at his studio.

She checked on that though, and, 'Hello, Zoltán,' she greeted him pleasantly, as it suddenly came to her that she'd do herself no good at all to 'demand' anything where he was concerned. Tact, she realised, might be the best ammunition to start with.

'*Szervusz, Arabella,*' he replied in kind, as they took their places at the table.

'Does that mean, hello?' she questioned, and, although she had no intention of allowing him through her guard, she was all at once totally disarmed when he smiled, and agreed that it was.

She turned from him to greet Frida as she arrived with the soup. By now Ella had taken to serving both herself and her host so she gave her attention to ladling *halászlé* into their dishes, and then concentrated on enjoying the clear fish and onion soup.

'Do you skate?' Zoltán, with that way he had of never saying anything at all like that which she supposed, did it again a little later when Frida had been in to clear and to set the next course on the table.

'Er—skate?' Ella queried, wondering what tack he was on now—or if he was suggesting that she take herself off skating somewhere.

'In December Lake Balaton freezes,' he replied.

'Enough to skate on?' she enquired, as he helped her to the main course.

'It is popular, as with ice sailing and sledging,' he informed her—and, more staggeringly, when she knew that she would be back in England long before Christmas, Ella suddenly felt that she wanted to be here when the lake froze over.

'Er—does this recipe have any special name?' she took a leaf out of his book to comment on something which they hadn't been discussing, as finding a strange need to get herself back together, she indicated the peppers stuffed with minced pork that accompanied some boiled potatoes and a home-made tomato sauce.

'*Töltött paprika,*' he answered, his glance steady on her. 'It is to your liking?'

'It's super,' she replied, and felt so much of a non-sense as she flicked a glance upwards and was pinned for a second by his thoughtful grey-eyed gaze that it took her until the next and final course for her to remember that she had intended to keep up a 'so when do I get to wear my ballgown?' offensive.

Frida had just brought in some of her delectable pastries and had gone out again when Ella decided that, since the meal was not yet over, she still had chance—so to speak—to lob one over his bows. So, apropos of nothing, but in the same way that he had been ready to instigate conversation with his 'Do you skate?' remark, 'I,' she looked up to bluntly state, 'am growing bored.'

Here we go, she thought when his expression immediately became icy, his look unfriendly, as she hadn't seen it in over a week. Zoltán fixed her with a cold scrutiny, and then clipped, 'Might I suggest, if that is the case, that you find yourself something to do?'

'How about sitting for my portrait, for one?' she flared, instantly stung. 'That's what I came here for!' she added heatedly. 'The rate things are going I'll be twenty-two before you set brush to...' She broke off when, her angry eyes following, Zoltán did no more than—clearly furious with her and her insolence—got up and strode angrily from the room.

Swine, she dubbed him, and, feeling suddenly that another morsel of anything to eat would choke her, she too left the room. Swine, swine, swine, she fumed as she stormed up the stairs; for two pins she'd return home to England.

She gained her room, and was still fumingly considering getting out her cases and making for the airport in Budapest with all speed when she suddenly realised, with no small mystification, that there were two very good reasons why she wouldn't be catching the first plane she could back to England. The one, that her father would, without question, go spare if she did anything of the kind. The other and, she had to admit, strangely the stronger reason of the two was that despite her fury—impotent rage and fury—with Zoltán Fazekas, she just did not *want* to leave. She simply didn't want to go! Now why the heck was that?

Ten minutes later, Ella had still not discovered what it was that pulled her to stay when, her pride and spirit up in arms, everything decreed that she should go. She was still puzzling at it when she donned a sweater and a jacket over her shirt and trousers and decided to go for a walk.

Could it have anything to do with the fact that Zoltán's home on Lake Balaton was situated in a most enchanting area? she wondered as she left her room. Piece by piece, during her conversations with Zoltán over this past week, she had learned that Lake Balaton was the largest lake in Central and Western Europe, and that it had over a hundred and twenty miles of shoreline. She had learned, too, that it had some long and sandy beaches in the south, but that Zoltán's home was on the north shore somewhere in between Badacsony and a village named Szigliget. Badacsony was apparently an area of extinct volcanoes and was a region which produced wines of some note from the volcanic soil on the hillsides. Szigliget, on the other hand was an ancient and picturesque village with its own castle ruins dating back to the thirteenth century.

But Ella gave her thoughts to other matters as she exited through the front door. Which way should she go? Either way was a longish walk, be it towards Szigliget or the road to Badacsony. Though, since the whole area was beautiful...

Undecided as she was, she thought to go and take a look at the lake from the rear of the house. She had been there before, and knew that the footpath from the rear led to a private jetty where a very sturdy-looking rowing boat and a couple of sailing dinghies were tied up.

She was halfway along the path, however, when propped up against a tree she spotted a bicycle. Oszvald, she realised must have been out somewhere and just come back in. She was just about to walk past the bicycle, however, when, with a return of some of her ire, she recalled Zoltán's cold 'find yourself something to do!' and she hesitated. She hadn't been on a bicycle for years, but, to her mind, to go for a bike ride surely came under the heading of finding yourself something to do!

Just then, and as if it was meant that she should borrow the bicycle, she saw Oszvald coming out of the kitchen door and heading towards the bicycle. If he was intending to put it away in a shed somewhere, then she did hope he wouldn't mind leaving it until later.

'*Szervusz*, Oszvald!' she greeted him, and, giving him a smile as she went over to his bike and took hold of the handlebars, 'Er—*kérek egy*—er...' she ran out of Hungarian before she got very far, and had to finish her 'Can I have a' beginning, with an English, 'a ride?'

She rather gathered he'd got the picture when, looking a little concerned to start with, he seemed to suddenly make up his mind that it would be quite all right for her to borrow his bike and he came and pushed the bicycle round to the front of the house for her.

'*Köszönöm*, Oszvald,' she thanked him, and wished that he would disappear while she made her first attempts to get mobile.

He stayed where he was, however, but she reckoned that she didn't do too badly in that he had no need to come and pick her out of the gravel and, after a couple of false starts, she was away. She would have liked to have waved to him but with the handlebars being much freer than she'd expected she decided that she'd be better employed holding on with both hands.

Fifteen minutes later, and she was wondering what she had been worried about. It's a doddle, she thought, and pushed the pedals round without any particular note of which direction she was going in.

She recalled that she had told Zoltán that she was bored, and felt a bit sorry about that. But, as she cycled on up hill and down, past beautiful woodlands, she was far from bored. Then she remembered how she had felt up in her room that she didn't want to leave Hungary, that she wanted to stay, and all of a sudden she was feeling most dreadfully confused.

Abruptly she switched her thoughts away from such matters that she couldn't then understand and, discovering that she had cycled into an area of a few cottages and a local inn, she decided to think of other things. A refreshing drink after her exercise wouldn't come amiss, she decided, and dipping a hand into her jacket pocket she found a stray note and realised that she had the means to quench her thirst.

A brief while later, having communicated that she'd like a long non-alcoholic drink, Ella opted to take her lemonade outside. The weather was not too warm, but she was hot from her ride, and she was just wondering how many miles she had pedalled when the only other customer around as far as she could tell decided to take his refreshment outside too, and came to the same table.

'You do not mind?' he enquired politely. 'I heard you speak some English, and I thought I should like to speak so as well.'

Ella surveyed the twenty-three or twenty-four-year-old man for a few moments, then concluded that the fresh-faced fair-haired young man represented no threat. And, if she'd read it right, all he wanted to do was to practise his English anyway.

'Please,' she invited, indicating with her hand that he should take a seat.

Within the next five minutes, she had learned that his name was Timót, and that he was a musician who had Mondays off most weeks. She in turn told him that her name was Ella and—regardless of the fact that Zoltán had looked far from friendly the last time that she had seen him—that she was staying with friends in the area for a while.

'You are enjoying my country?' he enquired, and Ella was straight back to her confusion of knowing that she was enjoying his country so well that she didn't want to leave it.

'Very much,' she replied, and, eager to get away from a subject that seemed to be tormenting her, 'What's that that you're drinking?' she asked off the top of her head.

'*Barack pálinkát,*' he answered and as Ella studied the clear liquid in his glass, 'Apricot brandy,' he translated and, plainly not thinking much of her lemonade, 'I will get you a glass,' he promptly offered, and was gone before she could call him back.

During his absence Ella fretted on whether or not she should insist on paying for her *barack pálinkát* when her new friend returned. It did seem a rather prissy thing to do, to make a fuss about paying, she thought, especially when she felt certain—just intuitively knew—that he wasn't trying to be fresh.

On the grounds that, for all she knew, *barack pálinkát* might be extremely expensive, she did offer, 'May I pay?' when he came back.

But, 'You are my guest,' he replied, so she said no more but sampled the pleasing brandy and hoped that its alcoholic content was not too high. Zoltán would just love it if the police rang him to say that she was drunk in charge of a bicycle, she thought drily when her imagination took a little flight of fancy. 'What do you do at work when you do not staying in Hungary with friends?' Timót enquired.

'I work in a shop,' she replied, but did not add for two days a week only.

The next fifteen minutes were spent with her new friend picking her brains with some English words he was unsure of, and with him acquainting her with the information that a country inn was called a *csárda*.

Ella then thought that it was time she made her way back. 'It's been very nice meeting you, Timót,' she led up to her goodbye, 'but I must go now,' she told him.

'If you are here next Monday, I see you again?' he asked, and smiled, and because there was no more pressure than that, and because he was such a pleasant person, Ella smiled too.

'Perhaps,' she answered, of the view that if nothing had happened in the portrait-painting department by the following Monday she'd be ready to make off with Oszvald's bicycle without bothering to wait to ask his permission. She was just about to add a final goodbye to the broadly smiling Timót, however, and get to her feet, when before she could make a move her attention was distracted by the sound of a car door being furiously slammed.

Casually she glanced over to where the sound had come from—and suddenly all words died in her throat. For there, looking absolutely thunderous, and heading her way, was the tall and menacing figure of Zoltán Fazekas!

Oh, grief, she thought, and knew she was in trouble before she took another breath. She had no idea why he was so angry but from the way his lips firmed as he tossed a fierce look at her empty *barack pálinkát* glass she could not but wonder if he imagined that she had been sitting there knocking them back for hours!

'You are ready to go home, Arabella?' he ignored her companion totally to demand, and Ella just knew that there'd be hell to pay if she dared to say 'No, I'm not.'

'This is——' From somewhere her basic good manners prodded her to introduce Timót. But, all too obviously, Zoltán was in no mood to have her introduce anyone.

'Good,' he cut her off abruptly. 'Then come!' and, for all the world as though she'd just agreed that she was ready to go he bent and placed a firm hand beneath her elbow and 'helped' her to her feet.

At that moment, fury broke in Ella too. She had no idea what it was that she'd done wrong, but who the devil did he think he was? Why she let him get away with it she didn't know. But, because as his guest she reckoned that she owed him more loyalty than she did her new friend, 'Bye, Timót,' she bade him, and was made more fuming angry when Zoltán wasted no time but steered her angrily towards his car. 'Oszvald's bike!' she protested when Zoltán opened the passenger door of his car. 'I'll ride back on his bike, thanks all the same!' she told her host snappily.

'You'll ride nowhere but in my car!' Zoltán snarled, and looked tough enough to manhandle her inside if she let out so much as another peep.

'I'm not drunk,' she stayed rooted to argue, 'and I'm not leaving the bicycle here!'

'I'll get it collected!' he rapped.

'That's not——'

'Are you going to get in?' he threatened menacingly.

For perhaps three stubborn seconds Ella stood toe to toe with him, her blue eyes flashing sparks as she glared into the fierce grey of his. Then, 'Damn you!' she whispered fiercely, and, suddenly overwhelmingly conscious that Timót must be watching these proceedings, she was suddenly taken by embarrassment—and got into the car. Zoltán followed suit.

Not that the chisel-faced swine by her side had been the least embarrassed, she fumed as he set the vehicle in motion and they sped off.

'Did you have to be so rude?' she suddenly flared, unable to keep her fury with him bottled in any longer.

'To you?' he barked.

'To Timót, the man I was with,' she corrected him angrily. 'I was in the middle of introducing——'

'You think I'm interested in formally knowing all the men you pick up in bars?' he, to her utter outrage hurled at her.

'*Pick up!*' she fairly shrieked. '*Bars!*' she yelled, and, turning beside herself in her seat to look at him, so wild had he made her that only by the grace of God did she not start lashing out at him with her fists, 'How d-dare you?' she spluttered.

He flicked a glance of intense dislike at her, but seemed in no way perturbed by her fury, 'I dare because while you're here in my country, in my home as my guest, I'm responsible for you!' he gritted.

'Responsible!' she flew incensed, and realising that he must have come purposely looking for her, 'I'm almost twenty-two!'

'You've arranged to see him again?' he snarled.

'I may!' she hurled back. 'Timót's a pleasant man, who——'

'I'm not remotely interested!' Zoltán cut her off icily, and as he turned the car into his drive it was not long before Ella was sampling some car-door slamming of her own.

The swine! The utter, outrageous, cantankerous swine, she fumed as she charged over the drive, found the door locked and fumed some more when she had to wait for him to come and open the door for her.

He was responsible for her, was he? she raged as without so much as a glance to him she marched over his threshold, along the hall and up the stairs—well, not for much longer! A guest in his home, was she? Well, stuff his hospitality, she was going back to England!

Ella stormed into her bedroom and in a whirlwind of activity, she got out her suitcases, slammed one of them down upon the bed and opened it prior to beginning her packing.

Then all at once as she turned from the bed and went to take a step to her wardrobe, she stopped dead—and knew that she didn't want to go. Suddenly as all the anger abruptly drained from her, yet even while her pride insisted that to leave was the only thing left open to her she knew that she couldn't go, that she *could not leave*.

And, as suddenly, she all at once knew why! Her mouth fell open with the shock of it, and an audible gasp escaped, as, feeling stunned, she went over to an antique bedroom chair of green and gold, and collapsed into it.

It couldn't be, she wanted to protest, but protesting was useless. The knowledge was now hers, indelibly so, and would not go away. She had earlier thought that part of her reason for wanting to stay was because it was easier to do so than to face her father's wrath if she went home with no portrait to follow. But she was now able to see that her father did not come into it. She had thought another part of her reason for wanting to stay was because of the enchantment of her surroundings— because of the charm of the area where Zoltán had his home. But it wasn't that either, beautiful though the area was. The reason she did not want to leave, in fact felt that she *could not* leave, Ella then knew, was because she, stupidly, idiotically, and quite unwanted by Zoltán, had fallen in love with him!

It was nearing eight o'clock when, her cases stowed away again, Ella looked at herself nervously in the mirror and wondered if her love for him showed. She felt as if she had grown up very quickly over the last few hours, but accepted then that while she knew that Zoltán would never love her—indeed, with some pain she recalled how on the drive back he had looked at her as though he positively disliked her—she also knew that she would stay on with him for as long as she could. The days were going to be bleak enough when, her portrait completed, she would return to England, having severed all hope of ever seeing him again.

How strange was life, she reflected as she left her room—only at lunchtime she had decided that she would badger and badger away at him until he got fed up and decided to make a start on her picture—if only to shut her up. And now, now that the reason why she so often felt all churned up and fluttering inside when she was with him had become plain, she was in no hurry at all for him to get started. In actual fact, it would suit her very well if he couldn't make a start for an age yet.

Her insides gave a flutter for which she now knew the reason—when, on entering the drawing-room, she saw that he was already there. Instantly then, though, she remembered that which knowledge of her love for him had sent out of her head—the fact that they had parted as raging enemies.

For a moment, as she looked to his dear wonderful face, Ella was completely stumped to know how she was supposed to greet him. But, when he had been equally furious, to her relief, he spoke first, and she was able to take her lead from his pleasant tone.

'Gin and tonic, Arabella?' he enquired evenly, to her gratitude the cold look gone from his eyes, a warmer look there she was pleased to see.

'Thank you—only a small one.'

'I didn't think you'd had too much earlier,' he brought their mutual fury straight out into the open to remark.

But, when earlier she might well have gone for him and told him that she should jolly well hope not, now, later, and in love, she saw what he said as holding a hint of an apology. 'I'll still only have a small one,' she smiled.

She saw his glance go to her smiling mouth and linger there—then he was turning away and going over to the drinks table. He came back to hand her a glass, and his charm sinking, 'Did anyone ever tell you that you're magnificent in a fury?' he enquired blandly.

She could well have told him that no one, but no one, had ever got her so riled up that she had come within an ace of punching them. But she was only too well aware now that, if her pride was to survive intact, she must watch her words. By no chance was she going to give him cause to perhaps wonder what was so different about him that he could disturb her so, or that he more than anyone could move her to near uncontrollable fury. So, 'According to my father, it goes with the red hair—the fury, I mean,' she murmured, and was happy that the subject was dropped when Frida came in to say that dinner was ready.

Though what she ate that night Ella never remembered, for she was much too busy watching every word she said lest, her recognition of her love still too new, she slipped up and gave herself away. But her meal must have tasted good, she realised, for she had finished her soup, and her main course, and was drinking a cup of coffee after her pudding, and as Frida left the dining-room Ella belatedly realised that she had been so busy with other thoughts that she hadn't given so much as a thought to Oszvald and his bicycle.

'Would you convey my apologies to Oszvald for me, please, that I didn't return his bike?' she asked Zoltán, feeling able to bring the subject up only because he himself had so freely referred to it earlier.

But she had invited his gaze upon her, and had to force herself to stay calm, even if inwardly she was jangling with nerves when for long moments he looked into her eyes. Then, 'You wish to take the blame when clearly the fault is mine?' he enquired.

And while her heart and mind cried, Oh, Zoltán, I love you so, her tongue pointed out quite pleasantly, 'I was the one who borrowed the cycle.'

Again he just looked at her for long moments, then, 'What a monster you must think me!' he exclaimed softly, and suddenly Ella started to feel much better inside about loving him.

'You want it in writing?' she asked, a shade cheekily, she had to admit, and loved him yet more when he laughed, that laughter extending to the amused grey eyes that were still on her.

Suddenly, though, his mood seemed to change and he flicked his glance from her. And there was no laughter in his eyes when next he looked at her. But, as she began to wonder if perhaps she had been too saucy, and if she had been mistaken and had imagined his laughter, his amusement, he abruptly stated, 'I've decided we'll start work on your portrait in the morning!'

Oh, no! she thought, she didn't want him to start—not for ages yet. 'You're starting—in the morning?' she repeated, somehow, she knew not how, managing to keep her thoughts from showing in her expression.

'You've some objection?' he queried coolly.

'None at all!' she replied sharply, fully prepared to lie her head off if need be. 'You can start now if you like!' She knew that her words were challenging, sharp, and that she was most likely asking for trouble, so supposed she couldn't complain when, as she began, 'Just——' she got her answer.

'You'd better have an early night,' he cut in crisply, 'I don't want to paint you with dark circles under your eyes.'

Her coffee finished, Ella got indignantly to her feet; love the swine she might, but by no circumstance was he going to walk all over her. 'I'll go now!' she told him tartly, but found more acid before she left with which to enquire, 'Do I wear my ballgown down to breakfast?'

For a split second she thought he was going to break out into a grin, but then realised that it must have been a trick of the light. Because his expression was un-smiling and serious when, 'Forget the ballgown,' he told her sternly.

'Forget it?'

'I propose to paint you wearing that green velvet dress you wore that evening we dined out,' he replied, and while her eyes were going huge, 'You can change into it after breakfast,' he decreed.

For a second or two Ella just stood and stared at him, then, 'You're the artist!' she told him snappily—and got out of there quickly before the smile that was building up in her could break.

For Zoltán to have remembered the dress which she had only worn once in his company must mean that she looked all right in it, didn't it? It must mean—mustn't it?—that he approved anyhow and—as a thrill of pleasure took her—must have really meant it when that night, as she'd come down the stairs, he had told her she was beautiful.

She climbed the stairs with her heart far, far lighter than it had been.

CHAPTER SEVEN

As soon as breakfast was over the following morning, Ella slipped back up to her room to change, then, with a feeling of excitement at the thought of spending long hours in Zoltán's sole company, she went to join him.

The studio to which he took her was on the top floor of his Lake Balaton home, and was a vast, light and airy room, and a window-cleaner's fortune, she thought, there was so much glass.

'Come and sit over here,' Zoltán instructed, and, indicating a carved wood-framed satin-backed couch, he walked over to it with her, waited until she was seated, then touched her arm to adjust her into the position he wanted. 'Your hands in your lap, I think,' he murmured, to Ella's relief, having no idea at all of how her wildly misbehaving heart fluttered most ridiculously just to have his hand touch the bare skin of her arm.

He took his time, his expression serious, until she was posed just how he wanted to paint her. Then, leaving her, he went over to where he already had a prepared canvas on a stand. From there he stood and looked, with a critical eye, she realised, over to where she was seated.

Then, 'You're sitting too stiffly,' he told her, and instructed, 'Relax, Arabella. You've a natural grace—try to relax.'

Ella liked that bit about 'a natural grace'; she hadn't been aware of it. She was aware, though, that she felt stiff and awkward, but try as she might she found she just couldn't be natural.

'I'm sorry,' she apologised; the last thing she wanted was that he should get angry with her for wasting his time. 'I'm trying, honestly, only I'm not used to...' She broke off, never having realised that 'just sitting', while trying to look 'natural', would be so difficult.

To her relief, however, Zoltán did not get angry with her but, to her joy, he actually smiled as he took up a piece of charcoal, and, as she realised that he was first going to sketch in some detail, he pleasantly suggested, 'Tell me some more about yourself, Arabella.'

'You already know most of what there is to know,' she replied with a light laugh.

'I'm sure I don't,' he denied, and continued, 'What would you normally be doing on a Tuesday morning around this time, were you not here?'

That was easy. 'Tuesday's a shop day,' she replied. 'I'd have been hard at it for over an hour by now.'

'You work in a shop? I thought you——'

'Oh, it's only for two days a week. It's run by a chari- table organisation, but they're always short of helpers, so...' She broke off when she saw that he looked quite shaken. 'What did I say?' she promptly asked.

'What can *I* say?' he answered. 'Sweet little Arabella, I believe I owe you one very big apology.'

'I like it!' she exclaimed, that 'sweet little Arabella' nearly her undoing. 'But why apologise, particularly?' she asked.

'Have you no memory of the time I accused you of living a life of petty detail?' he enquired.

'Vaguely,' she answered, her face now deadpan, but her eyes laughing.

'I think—er—minx, is the word I'm searching for,' the tall Hungarian, who previously had had no problem with the English language, remarked. But he went on seriously, 'From what I learned of you before, and what

I've just now learned, it seems to me there must have been some days when you worked yourself to a shadow!'

'I wouldn't say that,' she denied. But she had to grin when she added impishly, 'Though it's true that there have been occasions when I've felt too exhausted come evening to go out and enjoy myself.'

She loved it when he grinned too, and, at his instigation, they spent quite some time in discussing what, for her, constituted enjoying herself. Having revealed to him that she found enjoyment in the opera, ballet, the theatre, and picnics on a summer's day—and they hadn't touched on horse riding and the dozen and one other things she gained enjoyment from—Ella suddenly became aware that Zoltán had started work. Indeed, he had been at work with his charcoal for several minutes, she realised, and she realised something else as well— that she felt totally relaxed.

Was he something of a man or wasn't he? she thought fondly, knowing then that Zoltán had deliberately got her talking so that she would feel less stiff, and more able to relax.

The next hour went by with Zoltán taking his eyes off his work every now and then to look at her. At other times, he would stand completely back from his easel, and study what he'd so far done, and then study her once more. On her part, Ella found she had all the time in the world to study him, his features, the strong set of his jaw, his high intelligent forehead.

His concentration was total, yet he was aware of the smallest movement she made, she discovered. For when, having been conscious for the past ten minutes of her bones setting in one position, she just had to move a fraction, 'Keep still!' he rapped. But only to relent a little later to enquire, 'Would you like to rest?'

'No, thank you,' she replied, knowing that she might be being foolish but sensing that, Zoltán being an artist in full flow, it was important to stay with it and get on.

She thought she had got that right when he didn't argue, but carried on working away. Her thoughts floated about for a little while then and she found that she was wondering if other people who'd sat for Zoltán had been always asking if they could have a break. And it was then that she resolved that she would be quite unlike any of his sitters. She wouldn't ask for a rest once.

Nor, she thought, as she began to grow curious at that early stage about how her portrait was coming along, would she be forever asking if she could take a look. Well, she qualified, aware that she possessed something of an overlarge curiosity, not unless invited. She was somehow certain that all his sitters asked 'Can I look?' She, would be different.

Her decision not to ask if she could take a rest was sorely strained soon afterwards, though, and was only kept by a certain determination in her nature, for her bones began to feel more rigidly set than ever. The problem was, she realised, that she was more used to being on the move—it was hard work to sit frozen.

Zoltán had long since exchanged charcoal for brush when, her limbs screaming that she must have been sitting still like that for ten hours, *at least*, he looked over again, all the time, she guessed, taking in her position.

Since he had studied art, she surmised he must know by heart every bone in the human body. She realised then, though, that he must have suddenly spotted that there was something the merest fraction out of alignment in her posture, because all at once he stopped.

'We'll finish for now,' he informed her, going over to a large sink in the corner of the room, and, after first rinsing through the brush he'd been using, washing his hands.

This is when I say 'Can I look?' Ella thought, but, having resolved not to be like everyone else, stubbornly she wouldn't. 'What time is it?' she asked, her wrists bare of watch or jewellery.

'Almost one,' Zoltán obliged, and, while she was thinking, Was that all? he was coming over to her, stating, 'You should have stopped me!'

'Stopped you?'

'When you first began to feel as if you were creaking in every muscle,' he replied. 'Try gently stretching,' he suggested kindly, and when she did—and winced for the effort, 'Ah—it's got you between the shoulder-blades,' he detected, and knew what to do about that too.

A few seconds later he had come round to the back of the couch and, to make her heartbeats burst into energetic life, he had taken a hold of her shoulders and had begun to massage the knots out of her muscles.

Her dress was cut into a V at the back and as Zoltán massaged downwards in the most wonderful circular movements so Ella's skin started to tingle. Oh, heavens, she thought, and, as his touch did mindless things to her, heaven was what it was.

'Do you—do this, for all your clients?' she asked, while striving with all she had for a normal tone of voice.

'Only a favoured few,' he replied drily, and, unsure whether he was joking, Ella, as jealousy was born, knew that the favoured few would only be the beautiful ones.

Then jealousy was sent on its way when Zoltán found the centre of a knotted muscle in her left shoulder and 'Ooh!' she exclaimed.

'I'm sorry,' he apologised.

'Don't stop!' she pleaded, and such was the relief his touch gave that she was delighted when, in order to get closer to the awkward spot, he came round and sat on the couch with her.

'Here?' Zoltán asked, his fingers busy again.

'Wonderful,' she breathed, and, for a few moments, she closed her eyes.

When she opened them again, it was to find herself looking straight into his eyes, his warm steady grey eyes. She opened her mouth to say something, then her breath caught—and she was not conscious of breathing at all. For Zoltán was bending his head, coming closer, and she wasn't sure that she didn't move that bit closer to him. But while she could still feel one hand warm on her skin, slowly, giving her all the time she needed to back away if she felt so inclined, his other arm came about her. Then, gently, he kissed her.

'Oh, Zoltán!' she breathed when he broke that kiss. She saw him shake his head as though to clear it. But when his hold on her seemed to slacken and she realised that he was going to let her go, was going to pull back, some other part of her, the part without pride, made her cling on to him—and lean that little bit forward, offering him her lips.

She heard his muttered exclamation, then cared not what he'd muttered, because suddenly he was pulling her close up to him again, and once more his mouth was over hers.

Nor was that the only kiss they shared. Held tightly up against him, Ella pressed against him giving her lips freely, in love with him and burning with an ever growing passion.

'Sweet Arabella,' he murmured, and traced kisses down her face, to the base of her ears, down her throat and to the swell of her breasts.

'Zoltán,' she murmured his name in return, and was half sitting, half lying with him on the couch when he pushed the green velvet from her shoulders to touch his lips to the fine silk of her skin.

But her dress was restricting, and she had no objection at all to make when, with his lips once more over hers, his hands at the back of her unzipped her dress. Oh, my darling, darling, she wanted to cry out when in gentle and tender movements he brushed her dress all the way down her arms.

Ella kissed him as she took her arms from her dress, and knew yet more rapture when, her dress somewhere around her waist, she felt his warm sensitive hands on the skin of her naked back.

Again she wanted to cry out his name, and she clutched on to him tightly when, with more tender and gentle movement, he undid her bra and removed it.

She had moved to sit up a little in order to help him with her clothing, but as his artist's hands caressed her back, and then gently, caringly, they caressed to the front of her until at last his hands were caressing her full and throbbing breasts, so Ella gripped him yet more tightly.

'Zoltán!' she cried his name again, could not help herself, when, as ever gentle with her, he traced kisses down to the hardened peaks of her breasts and then captured each one in turn between his lips, before tracing tender kisses down the valley between these twin silken globes. Gently, then, he raised his head, and kissed her lips.

And Ella, thought that she would deny him nothing. Indeed *knew* that she would deny him nothing. She loved him, was in love with him and, regardless of her highly moral upbringing, her love for Zoltán transcended everything else. If he wanted her, and she knew that he did, then she was his.

Though first she had to overcome an unexpected moment of shyness. How she should feel shy when, with her dress somewhere around her middle, she was willingly allowing Zoltán to kiss every naked part of her, she couldn't have said. But all at once as he leaned back as though to gaze in full at her uncovered breasts so she experienced a moment of agitation. It was a reflex action she could do nothing about that caused her to jerk her arms from around him and to use her hands to try to conceal herself from his gaze.

But, even while she at once regretted what she had done, Ella just the same found she seemed to have seized up, and just then could not remove her covering hands. Sorely needing help, she looked up—and straight into Zoltán's warm grey gaze.

'Ah!' he breathed softly, and oh, so gently, his eyes holding hers, his hands came to her wrists and he leaned forward and planted a whisper of a kiss on first one cheek, and then the other. Then for a moment he pulled back to look into her eyes, then gently took her hands away from her breasts, and, while keeping his eyes quiet on hers for a moment or two longer, he then transferred his gaze to her naked and throbbing with her need for him breasts. 'You're oh, so—so beautiful,' he murmured, and raised his glance to her pinkened face.

'Oh, Zoltán!' she cried a little shakily, and didn't know where she was when he bent to place a tender kiss on first her right breast and then her left, and then, raising his head, he planted a whisper of a kiss on her mouth.

'Never be afraid of me, little one,' he breathed, his voice reaching her as thick and husky in his throat, and while Ella wanted to cry out that she wasn't afraid of him, she wasn't, he had found her bra and was putting her into it. And all before she knew it, while a fire for him was still raging in her body, she was back inside her green velvet dress and was neatly zipped up and if there was a fire still raging inside him he was manfully controlling it, because he commented mildly, 'Perhaps massaging the stiffness out of your shoulders was not such a good idea, after all.'

Ella felt choked. She wanted to protest, 'You can't behave this way, leave me wanting you this way. You did it. You awakened this burning force in me—and now...' But something else had awakened in her—that pride which only a short while ago she had misplaced.

'All part of getting to know me, I'm sure!' she murmured, trying desperately hard for a dry note—only to find that her voice had come out with a tart edge to it.

'I know that you're a virgin,' he replied, 'and that *is* for sure.'

Her breath caught in her throat, 'How?' she demanded, but all she received by way of a reply was a grin. And she loved his grin, and she loved him—and she seriously needed to be on her own so that she could get her head back together. 'Do I—come back this afternoon?' she queried, her eyes on the door as she got to her feet.

Zoltán did nothing to detain her but got to his feet also and even walked over to the door with her and opened it for her, 'I can work without you this afternoon,' he answered pleasantly, and as she stepped out on to the landing the firm closing of the door behind her told her that she was alone.

Sorely then did she need something solid to lean on, but common sense was struggling to be heard and instead of leaning heavily against the wood panelling of the door Ella went swiftly down the stairs and along to the far landing to her room.

She was trembling, she discovered as she sank down into a bedroom chair and tried for some semblance of normality. But nothing was normal any more. Zoltán had kissed her passionately, and had been on the way to making complete and wonderful love to her, had been on the way to taking her, making her his—and she would have let him, welcomed him! How could things ever be normal again after that?

For minute after minute Ella sat where she was, but she was feeling little better for her cogitations when she left her chair, to get out of her green dress and to shake it and to hang it up for the creases to fall out.

It *had* happened, Zoltán had kissed and caressed her and taken her briefly to an enchanted land, but that was an end to it. All too clearly his detached attempt to massage the knots out of her tied-up muscles had suddenly and unexpectedly lost its detachment. And, while she hoped and prayed with everything in her that she had given away nothing in those early stages of what his touch was doing to her, she faced honestly the fact that she could not regret what had happened. To be enfolded in Zoltán's arms had been bliss, pure bliss—so how could she regret it?

Ella thought she had come to know a little of the man to whom she had given her heart, and as she acknowledged that it had just never been in his mind to set out to seduce her, and that what had happened had just—happened, so she knew that it would never happen again. Zoltán, she realised, would make certain of that.

Which, she decided, was perhaps just as well. By her response to him Zoltán must know that she found him attractive but—and to save her pride—that was a long, long way from his knowing that she was in love with him.

Feeling all strung-up still, Ella ceased walking the floor and glanced at her watch to note that there were only a few minutes to go before two o'clock. She wasn't in the least hungry, she owned as she put on some speed to get into some smart trousers and a light sweater. But, since

Frida had gone to the trouble of making a meal, it was only courteous that she went down and sat at the table.

'*Szervusz*, Frida.' She found a smile from somewhere for the housekeeper who was in the dining-room waiting for her when she went in. She would have liked to have asked her how her rheumatism was that day, but knew that her Hungarian was by no chance up to putting such a question. '*Bocsánat a késésért*,' she apologised for being late instead, and felt warmed by the other's beaming smile on her efforts anyway to get her tongue around the Hungarian language.

Warmth and smiles departed from Ella, however, when the housekeeper left the room. Zoltán was not coming down to lunch, then! Somehow, when she had just inwardly known that this lunchtime would be one of those lunchtimes when she would see nothing of him, Ella felt disappointed. Oh, lord, was it always going to be like this?

Ella did her best to do justice to the meal which Frida had prepared, and felt worse than ever to realise that what she was going to feel would be worse than disappointment when she left Hungary. For, once she was back in England, she would have lost all chance of bumping into him at a mealtime.

Restlessly she got up from her chair and returned to her room. But to stay pacing her room all afternoon wasn't what she wanted either, she realised as the restlessness persisted. Within the next couple of minutes, she was jacket-clad and was running lightly down the stairs.

Instinctively she turned to the rear of the house and didn't know that she was looking for sight of Oszvald's cycle until she stood staring at the tree it had been propped up against yesterday—and realised that it wasn't there.

Guiltily she wondered if Oszvald's bike had been returned to him yet. But, although she was feeling in the need for some activity, it was that feeling of guilt—that she had been the one to borrow it yet had returned without it—that stopped her from going and asking, if it was back, could she borrow it again.

Never more unsettled, she wandered down to the jetty and stood staring out at the wind-rippled green waters of the lake. She was, however, in the middle of solemnly mentally photographing everything in her mind's eye to remember when she was back in England when she suddenly picked up the sound of footsteps coming in her direction.

She half turned around, but as colour surged to her face as she saw Zoltán, trouser-and-sweater-clad, step on to the jetty and start walking towards her so she swiftly turned back to look at the lake.

She was desperately racking her brains for something cool, and if possible, sophisticated to say to him but, her mind a blank of anything cool or sophisticated, she could only love him more when he came and stood beside her, and asked affably, 'How's Arabella?'

A smile that reached right down to the tip of her toes began inside her. 'Fine, thanks,' she returned. 'How's Zoltán?'

She didn't get to hear his answer because he had gone a few yards away from her and had climbed into one of the dinghies moored at the jetty. She had a vague notion of reading somewhere that men enjoyed messing about in boats, but had to own that it was a pleasure watching him do exactly that.

Quite suddenly though, she realised that he was erecting a sail, and, 'I thought you were working this afternoon!' burst from her.

He looked up, his glance friendly on her as she stood long-legged, straight-backed and flame-haired, 'Slave-driver!' he accused, and got on with what he was doing.

'You're going out?' she enquired swiftly, when a moment later she saw that he looked about to depart—surely there was room enough for two in that boat!

'I thought I might,' he drawled casually.

'Oh,' she murmured, and just could not ask him to take her with him.

She watched as he seemed to have finished doing all that needed to be done. Then he stood and looked over to where she was standing. Then, a hint of a smile quirking up the corners of his mouth, he invited, 'Well?' and at his smile, that lovely friendly light in his eyes, Ella waited no longer.

'I thought you'd never ask,' she grinned saucily, and took but a second to cross the dividing space and trust-ingly put her hands out to take hold of the ones he held up to help her down into the boat.

She found his touch burning, but he dropped her hands as soon as she was settled and enquired, 'Ever sailed before?'

'Never,' she replied, and listened intently while he in-structed her on a few dos and don'ts, then he was re-leasing the dinghy from its mooring—and they were away.

Over the next hour they sailed and tacked and skimmed over the water—and Ella loved every moment of it. There was more wind out on the lake than she had thought, and it was much colder too than she'd ima-gined, but nothing could mar the thrill and enjoyment of it all.

'Do you think you'll like it?' Zoltán teased at one stage, when with her hair streaming out behind her she turned her face up to the sky in obvious exhilaration.

She guessed she had no need to answer, any confirmation he needed that she found sailing a delight there to be seen. Indeed, so enraptured was she that she felt quite downcast when Zoltán said that they would return home.

'Already?' she protested. 'We've only been out five minutes.'

'Sixty-five to be exact,' he replied, 'and it's cold.'

Ella felt sure that it wasn't on his own account, because of his feeling cold, that they were going in. But she was highly sensitive where he was concerned, and, although she would dearly have liked to have protested that she wasn't in the least cold, she thought she had protested enough by letting him know that sixty-five minutes in his company had seemed like only five.

Her feeling of happiness and exhilaration was still with her, though, as she walked back along the jetty with him. Her head was still half filled with the fantastic experience of gliding over water under sail, when on their way to the house they passed by the tree where she'd seen Oszvald's bike parked yesterday, and, 'Did you get Oszvald's bike back to him?' she enquired innocently—and was totally stunned to have her happy and exhilarated mood promptly stamped on.

'You were thinking of taking a ride to your friend at the *csárda*?' Zoltán snarled toughly.

'What a good idea!' she flared, and stormed away from him, at that instant feeling that she hated Zoltán Fazekas because with a few short words he could so utterly spoil for her her feeling of joy.

She did not go in search of the cycle or in search of her new friend, Timót, though he was more acquaintance than friend, she felt, when up in her room she railed against Zoltán. Hell's teeth, was there ever such a man? Never had she known any one who could play ducks and drakes with her temperament the way he could.

An hour later she lay having a soak in the bath and was much calmer. She had no need to look further than Zoltán's backing off this morning when, his for the taking, he—somehow aware that she was a virgin—must have remembered that she was in his safe-keeping. Hadn't he implied something of the sort yesterday when he'd said that while she was under his roof she was *his* responsibility? Hence his getting tough not so long ago when it occurred to him that she might want to take another bike ride to the inn.

By the time Ella was ready to go down to dinner that night, though she still felt annoyed with Zoltán for ruining her idyllic mood, she was so much in love with him that she decided to put her annoyance behind her. When she returned to England she wanted only pleasant memories and not memories of her and Zoltán rearing up at each other.

To her delight, his mood was back to being affable when she joined him for a pre-dinner drink. It remained so as they strolled in to dinner and, long before the first course was over, she was ready to forgive him anything.

The main course that evening was *debreceni tokány* which, among other things, consisted of smoked bacon, smoked sausage, beef, onions, peppers, paprika and tomatoes. It was served with rice and parsley potatoes, and was delicious. But they were nearing the end of that course, during which they had just been talking quite pleasantly on the matter of dancing, and their mutual liking for certain dance music, when Zoltán abruptly asked, 'You have many dance partners, Arabella?' and the abruptness of his tone warned her that pleasantness was wearing thin.

'Of course,' she replied lightly, seeing no need whatsoever to lie. She was a good dancer and, without conceit, since she didn't have a face like the back of a bus, she never had lacked for dance partners.

Zoltán's grunt was sufficient indication for her to know that he was displeased about something. For one fantastic heart-fluttering moment it crossed her mind that—could it be?—he was jealous! She immediately scrapped any such notion. A man of his sophistication—was it likely?

Frida had been in to clear away and bring in dessert before Zoltán spoke again, and then it was only to coolly ask, 'Your men friends—you have one in particular?'

'One in particular?' she enquired, wondering what track he was on now.

'One you date more than any other. One with whom you have a regular date?' he elucidated.

If he was asking was she going steady, then she wasn't. But, as Ella considered how to reply, she couldn't help but panic at the thought—had Zoltán that morning glimpsed a hint of the fact that she was in love with him? She felt hot all over as she wondered if his question, as well as being all part of an artist's needing to know what made his subject tick, did not have some kind of hope behind it that she was emotionally involved with someone else.

'I ride horses almost every Saturday with Jeremy Craven,' she replied at last, which was no lie, though she purposely left out the information that Jeremy's family were glad of any exercise for the horses they could get.

'And do you see this horse-riding friend regularly at other times too?' Zoltán wanted to know.

Ella did not like it that the cool look that had been in his eyes when she had first met him was there again.

But pride was at stake here, and she replied blithely, 'Oh, yes. There's always somewhere to go, something to do. Dinner, the theatre,' she added airily, this time omitting to mention that she and her friends normally went out in a crowd, or that Jeremy was just like another brother to her.

When she might well have gone on, though, she glanced at Zoltán and decided against it. Quite clearly, from the aloof expression on his face, he was utterly bored with the topic.

Ella finished her pudding in silence. Though she was sipping her coffee and was of the opinion that, if she bored him so much, she'd cut out her tongue before she'd say another word, when her curiosity, ever on the alert, chose that moment to plague her.

Zoltán hadn't held back from asking her about *her* friends of the opposite sex—she played with the idea for a moment or two. So, given that she would love to know all that there was to know about him but was not in the process of putting his likeness down on canvas, she just the same felt that he could have no quibble should she ask him about *his* friends of the opposite sex. She remembered the first night she had been in his Budapest home—he'd gone out after dinner that night. Ella didn't doubt that it had been to meet some lady.

'How about you?' she enquired, the question coming out more starkly than she had meant it.

Casually Zoltán let his gaze rove over her. 'Me?' he queried.

She wanted to swallow, but wouldn't. 'Do you date one woman more than any other?' she was bold enough to ask, and somehow, at the alert look that came to his eyes, wished that she hadn't.

For long moments then, he looked steadily at her, then, his gaze still intent upon her, 'Forgive me, Arabella, I'm not a kiss and tell man,' he drawled, and, while she was remembering the passion of the kisses they exchanged only that day, she suddenly went from very hot to icy cold when he all at once continued, 'Though it's common knowledge among those who know me well that one person special to me is a lady named Szénia Halász.'

Oh, how she wished that she hadn't asked! How she kept herself from crumbling to know that there was a 'special' woman in his life Ella never knew. Jealousy seared through her. Yet, somehow—pride, she later realised—she managed to appear outwardly as though the information he had just given her was of no consequence to her whatsoever.

But, some reply called for, she felt, 'I didn't mean to be rude. You didn't mind my asking?' she managed politely.

'Not at all,' he returned, equally politely—and there was no further conversation after that.

Not many minutes later, Ella excused herself and went up to her room. She felt beaten and, as jealousy took another nip, she wanted to go home. At the same time, however, she knew that she did not want to go home— did not want to sever that final link with Zoltán until she had to.

An hour later she climbed dispiritedly into bed, and, going over every word, look, and deed of that evening, she once more recalled the definite coolness that had been there when she and Zoltán had said goodnight.

She put out her bedside lamp, and lay staring into the darkness. Somehow, she had an unhappy and solid feeling that any empathy she had imagined between them was gone, forever.

CHAPTER EIGHT

ELLA got out of bed dispiritedly on a Friday morning reflecting that it was two and a half weeks since she had learned the name of Zoltán's favourite female—and everything seemed to have fallen apart since then. The name of Szénia Halász was burned in her brain, and, although Ella was at pains that Zoltán should know none of the jealousy that racked her over his lady-love, she supposed that her efforts to appear entirely unconcerned might well be seen as—uncaring.

Not that that mattered particularly, she thought unhappily as she went to get bathed. Anything was preferable than that he should know that care, she very much did. Though it was true, she had to accept, that he didn't appear to be one tiny bit bothered how she felt about him.

As she'd suspected, all sign of any feeling of empathy between them had gone. She sat, in silence, most mornings while he continued with her portrait. Her afternoons were free while he continued with work for which he did not require her to be there. Never again though did he come anywhere close enough to lay so much as one single massaging finger on her person. And, while she of course knew that since the last time he'd thought to relieve the stiffness in her muscles passion had flared, it didn't help to make her feel any better to know that she could be solidified with excruciating pain before he'd come to her aid again.

Ella later left her room to go slowly down the stairs not knowing quite how long it took to have one's portrait painted, but aware by then that for certain she couldn't hope to stay in Hungary for much longer.

'Good morning,' she greeted Zoltán civilly on entering the breakfast-room and swiftly turned her gaze from him to greet the hovering housekeeper. '*Jó reggelt,* Frida,' she smiled, and, while she was pleased to see that the housekeeper no longer seemed troubled by her rheumatism, Ella took her place at the table with an otherwise heavy heart.

In silence she drank the coffee which Zoltán poured for her, and in silence she ate the toast which Frida had brought—and wished with all she had to have those days back when, the atmosphere warmer, Zoltán had sometimes been amused by something she'd said, and, in turn, sometimes made her laugh.

But those days seemed to be gone for ever and she...she knew that she was beginning to feel the strain. 'Studio in fifteen minutes?' she queried coolly, if politely, breakfast over.

For long unspeaking moments Zoltán looked coldly at her. Then, 'I'm not working today,' he announced.

'You're not...' Her voice tailed off.

'The light isn't good enough,' he stated bluntly, and she was reminded of how, twice that week—after studying her for some while—Zoltán had abandoned work in the studio, declaring, when the light had seemed perfect to her, that the light was no good for what he wanted to achieve.

'You know best, I'm sure,' she muttered stiffly.

'I'm glad you appreciate it,' he replied loftily. Abruptly she got to her feet but, as she swung round to leave the room. 'But, to save you from growing bored,' he delayed her to throw one of her earlier comments back at her, 'I'll take you for a drive around.'

Ella halted. There was nothing she would like better than to go for a drive around with him. But, such was the perversity of love, that, 'You don't have to—I can easily borrow Oszvald's bike and go for a...' Her voice trailed off when Zoltán angrily pushed his chair back.

'Be ready in half an hour!' he ordered her curtly, and, as he strode past her and from the room, that, she saw, was the end of the matter!

Twenty-nine minutes later she surveyed her jacket-and-trouser-clad self in her bedroom mirror, and while trying to deny an inner turmoil that she was going out for a drive with Zoltán—be it only to keep her from growing bored—decided that her outfit was about right for a chilly October day.

With a woollen scarf draped casually around her neck, Ella descended the stairs just as casually. Her heart might have started drumming to beat the band when she saw that Zoltán was at the bottom of the stairs waiting for her, but only she was going to know of it.

'Right on time, you see!' She smiled as she joined him, wanting with all she had to get back to their old footing. And for one marvellous moment, as a warmer look than she was used to seeing of late entered his eyes, she thought that they might start out on their drive a little more friendly than they had been.

Just at that moment though, Lenke suddenly appeared to speak with him, was answered, and, as the maidservant went away, so Ella knew a feeling of dreadful disappointment. For all sign of him being amicably disposed to her had disappeared when, cold-eyed and curt, 'There's a phone call for you!' he grated, and, as she stared at him, startled, he clipped, 'Take it in my study!' and strode from her in the direction of a room which she by then knew was his study.

To her surprise, though, he did not at once leave the study so that she could take her call in private, but stood right there at her elbow while she picked up the telephone and said 'Hello?' into the instrument.

'Is that you, Ella?' asked the well-remembered voice of her dear brother.

'David!' she exclaimed in pleased delight, and, even while she was aware of the irritated movement of the man by her side, 'How lovely to hear you! How are you?' she asked.

'Terrific!' he replied, and sounded more cheerful than she had ever heard him when, 'Absolutely terrific!' he added, and went on, 'You've been away ages—when are you coming back?'

'I'm coming home soon!' she replied, and, even while she wondered how she'd managed to sound so cheerful herself when she found the very thought of returning to England and leaving Zoltán so terrible, she heard the impatient sound that came from her host the moment before he swung about and slammed out of the room.

'Good!' David opined, going on, 'I particularly want you here for the ceremony. That's why I'm ringing, actually. I've had the devil's own game getting your phone number, by the way. The one Father's got is for an address in——'

'Ceremony?' Ella cut in. 'What ceremony?'

'Of course, you don't know. Viola and I are getting married!' he cried excitedly.

'You are!' Ella exclaimed. 'Congratulations!' she wished him enthusiastically. 'You finally got Viola to say yes, then?'

'Silly love, she wanted to marry me all along, she's since told me. It was just that, what with the baby and everything, she was just being sticky because, the daft darling, she didn't want me to think that I *had* to marry her.'

They chatted away for another minute or so, then, 'So—when's the wedding?' Ella asked.

'Next month!' David replied promptly. 'As soon as Mother gets back.'

'Mother doesn't know yet?'

'Not yet. She's phoned, but that was ages ago before everything was sorted out. Luckily Father wasn't in, so I just told her that we were all fine and to carry on enjoying her holiday.'

'You can be very nice when you try,' Ella teased him gently.

'Nuts!' he replied. 'You just be here next month, that's all!'

Ella left the study in a sombre frame of mind. She had earlier realised that her portrait would soon be finished anyway, her reason for staying on under Zoltán's roof gone. Now, with David getting married, she was going to have to leave soon anyhow. With the unhappy knowledge that once she left she would never again return, she went in search of Zoltán.

She found him sitting in his car, the engine running, and with not a smile in sight. Great, she thought, that just matches my mood, and climbed in beside him.

It was a foregone conclusion, she later realised, that the drive around would not be much of a success. While on the one hand she could not help but be pleased and delighted for her brother that, in marrying Viola Edmonds, David would be gaining his heart's desire, it only served on the other hand to show her that she hadn't a hope of attaining hers. She and Zoltán were barely speaking, so fat chance of him ever falling in love with her.

Fat chance of the drive around lasting for very long either, Ella thought when, well in time for lunch, Zoltán turned the car around and headed back.

As a drive out it had been fairly informative, Ella thought glumly, by then acquainted with the peninsula of Tihany, a wide stretch of land that jutted far out into Lake Balaton to about only a mile away from the opposite shore.

Tihany, Zoltán had unbent sufficiently to inform her, had been declared a national park in 1952. There was a twin-spired church of some note in Tihany village, the eighteenth-century Benedictine Abbey Church, and Zoltán showed her round its baroque art monuments and took her down to the crypt where King Andrew, who had laid its original foundations in the eleventh century, was buried—then they were back in the car, and returning the way they had come.

'That was most interesting,' Ella retained her manners to thank him once he had stopped and she got out of the car.

His answer was to ignore her and to steer his car into the garage, and Ella went into the house and up to her room knowing that, were things different between them, she would thoroughly have enjoyed her trip to the Tihany Peninsula.

She did not see Zoltán at lunch, but while she longed to see him she had not the slightest intention of asking where he was. Since, to her, however, the light appeared to be no better than it had, she doubted that he was working. She spent the afternoon in her room determinedly writing letters.

Jealousy was rife in her, however, when, as he had twice last week, Zoltán dined elsewhere. He was not at the table for dinner anyhow and Ella found her jealousy no easier to cope with for knowing the name of the female whom she was certain was sitting across some dining table from him that evening.

She went to bed early, slept badly, and didn't feel at all better for her early night come morning. 'Good morning,' she greeted Zoltán with dedicated cheerfulness when she went down to breakfast. She'd die before she'd let him know that thoughts of him with Szénia Halász had kept her sleepless.

'Good morning, Arabella,' he returned, he too seeming to be making an effort to put some lightness into the atmosphere.

Either that, or after his date with Szénia Halász last night he was feeling so light-hearted he wasn't having to try, Ella thought sourly some while later. She was feeling more than a little downcast at the thought when, dressed in her green velvet, she was seated on the satin-backed couch in his studio. Being in love, she decided unhappily, was murder. Hoping that Zoltán might one day care for her in some small way was useless, she felt, and sighed—and nearly jumped out of her skin when he spoke sharply.

'Something is wrong, Arabella?' he asked abruptly.

'Wrong?' she queried startled, and saw his lips compress. From her expression, she guessed, it had been plain that her thoughts were not of the most gladsome. 'Er...' She hesitated, playing for time as she realised that she wasn't going to make things any better by denying that there was anything wrong. 'I was—er—thinking of home,' she quickly invented.

'You feel an urgent need to return after your phone call yesterday?' he rapped shortly. Oh, lord, Ella thought, and knew a feeling of having graduated with honours in the subject of not being able to do a thing right!

She shrugged—it took a mammoth effort. Then fear rushed in that Zoltán might not wait until he had finished her portrait but decide that if she wanted to return home so urgently he could finish it without her. 'Actually,' she rushed on in her fear that he would send her away, 'I was—more—wondering if the trouble at home had blown over yet.'

Zoltán, she observed, didn't look any less aggressive, but nor was he ordering her to take the next plane to England. 'The trouble your brother is in from your father?' he enquired, having apparently not forgotten what she'd told him weeks ago.

'It—er—sometimes takes an age for the dust to settle,' she agreed, discovering to her further unhappiness that—when she knew full well that the trouble at home had blown over, for David would never have sounded so cheerful, despite everything, if her father was still giving him hell—she was having the hardest work to lie to Zoltán. She gained strength, however, from knowing that the alternative would be untenable. Zoltán had picked up that her thoughts had not been happy ones. Anything was preferable than that he should guess her unhappiness stemmed from the fact that he would never love her.

'What sort of trouble is your brother in?' he, to her surprise, questioned. But although she instinctively knew that she could confide anything in him she discovered she just could not perpetuate the lie about her brother still being in trouble.

Which left her only one alternative, and that was to reply, 'It's a—er—family matter,' which, she at once knew from the harsh look that came to his features, Zoltán had interpreted as her as good as saying mind your own business. 'I . . .' she hurried to apologise.

But, 'Keep your head still!' he ordered her sharply—and said not another word to her until about an hour and a half later he went over to the sink in the corner of the room and tossed over his shoulder, 'Go now.'

Her curiosity to see how her portrait was coming along had been taken to the limits of late. Particularly since it had occurred to her many times that by seeing at what stage her picture was she might perhaps be able to gauge how much longer she would be able to stay with Zoltán. But since not once had he invited her to take a look—indeed, he seemed by then not to expect her to step from her couch to his easel—and since too she had no wish for him to think her vain, it was now a point of principle not to meander over unless invited.

That being so, Ella left her couch without so much as another word, and returned to her room. And from then on, when she saw Zoltán neither at lunch nor dinner, in fact not at all after she left his studio, she spent the worst day of her life.

Ella got up on Sunday morning and was more inwardly churned up than ever. Pride declared, indeed insisted, that she go home immediately. But love, she again discovered, was far stronger than pride, and she owned that she was aching for sight of the man she loved. Even while hating him because he could again have been with some special female friend last night, Ella admitted she wanted to see him.

'Are we working today?' she greeted him when she entered the breakfast-room and, having hurt for the sight of him, feasted her eyes anywhere but on him.

'You would rather not?' he clipped, and, even as Ella wondered if he was looking for a fight, his tone drew her to look at him.

'It's Sunday,' she commented, should he have forgotten. 'But you've worked on a Sunday before, so if you've no pressing appointment,' or even if you have, she thought fiercely, 'then I'm quite happy to sit...'

'You're in a hurry for me to finish?' he questioned curtly, and Ella counted to ten.

'I didn't think artists hurried for anyone,' she remarked pleasantly, and feeling, incredibly, very much like breaking a few of his important fingers, she queried, 'I'll pour my own coffee, shall I?' and found control, despite being goaded beyond limits, in busying herself with the coffee-pot.

It was not an auspicious start to the day, but an hour later she was once more green-velvet-clad and seated in his studio. She was, by then, feeling much more collected, but the fact that she had felt goaded enough to have had such horrendous thoughts was a fair indication to her that the strain she was under was beginning to tell.

She saw Zoltán pause in his work to look at her before he made another brush stroke, and she made her face as expressionless as possible. She was still on her guard that his clever artist's eyes did not see into what went on in her heart.

The minutes ticked by and it was somewhere around noon when, with Zoltán looking across at her every so often, the thought that he might have come anywhere near to seeing that he meant so much to her was sufficient to make her suddenly panic. And, as again he looked over to her and again studied her before once more putting brush to canvas, so the words rushed to her lips to tell him that she was leaving.

Just then, though, before her lips had done more than part, a knock sounded on the wood panelling of the door, and an apologetic Frida came in. Since it was unheard-of for the housekeeper to interrupt her master when he was working, Ella guessed that Frida's visit must be on a matter of some importance.

A moment later Zoltán was addressing his housekeeper in his own tongue, and as Frida hurriedly replied, and Ella caught the word *telefon*, so she had the dreadful feeling that David was on the phone again. Oh, heck, she thought, and, while more than happy to chat with her brother any time, she was all too well aware that Zoltán—who did not seem very cheefully disposed towards her that day—was just going to love it if he had to break off, and wait, while she took a phone call from England!

But suddenly her tuned-in ears picked up the name 'Halász' and, as a sick feeling hit the pit of her stomach, so she knew that she didn't have to brace herself for Zoltán's wrath. The call wasn't for her—it was for *him*! And, from the smart way he put down his brush after hearing what Frida had to say, and began striding to the door, far from being annoyed to have his work interrupted, he seemed eager to have it interrupted by she of the Halász name.

At the door, though, he halted, and seemed to belatedly remember that he had another female sitting and awaiting his attention. 'I have to take a phone call—we will finish for today,' he instructed—and was gone!

I know you have to take a phone call, and who from, Ella fumed, but as she glared at the door after him she felt on the very brink of tears.

Don't be ridiculous, she sniffed at the very idea, but as jealousy gouged deeper into her unhappy soul she felt in need of urgent action, and left the couch. She was going home, she decided, as she crossed to the door. She was going back to England. She'd had it.

Feeling something akin to desperation, Ella had made it to the door when she turned for one last look at

Zoltán's studio, the place where he worked. Slowly, if with some agitation, she let her gaze rove the room. It came to rest on the canvas that stood on the easel where Zoltán had been working—and became glued there, until, everything else in the room fading into the background, she slowly began to walk over to it. It was as though someone else was in charge of her as Ella went over—and just had to satisfy her curiosity of these past weeks.

She rounded the easel, anticipating to look her fill. And indeed, she did just that. But, to her absolute amazement, *nowhere* could she see a likeness of herself!

Witlessly and for many stunned long seconds, Ella stood and gazed at the oil-painting on the easel. It was a landscape!

It was a brilliant landscape of some genius, she could tell that—but nowhere in there was there a figure that remotely resembled a human shape, or a face that remotely resembled her.

Needing to clear her head, Ella looked away, and back again—but it was still the same picture. She recalled the many times that morning when Zoltán had looked across at her before adding another brush stroke—and, since clearly this picture wasn't the result of only a morning's work, the way he had yesterday looked over to her in the same fashion.

Now why would Zoltán look at her—yet paint something entirely different? Something that wasn't even a portrait! Ella was still shaken to the depths of her being by her discovery, though had in no way come up with any suitable answer, when she left the studio.

Her feet seemed to take her automatically to her room, where she changed out of her velvet dress and into trousers and a warm sweater. She was still puzzling at it, her decision to leave for England at once relegated to second priority, when, barely aware what she was about but acting on an instinct that refused to allow her to be still, she left her room and went quickly down the stairs. At the bottom of the stairs she went to turn to the right, but, catching sight of the study, and knowing that the man she loved was in there talking to his favourite woman on the phone, she turned quickly to the left, and the outside door.

Ella wasn't quite sure what she was thinking of as she hurried down the rear path and to the jetty beyond. But her mind was a jumble of thoughts about that picture that wasn't her picture and how Szénia Halász was special to Zoltán, but how she would never be, when she suddenly realised that she was standing on the jetty looking out to the wind-ruffled waters of Lake Balaton.

From the lake her glance fell to the nearby dinghy, the one which Zoltán had taken her out in—in what seemed a life-time ago. She had been happy then, she recalled, and saw without really seeing that someone, either Zoltán or Oszvald, had been out in the boat fairly recently. There were sails in the boat, anyway, she saw, and as memory of that happy sixty-five minutes she had spent that day with Zoltán came back to her again Ella stepped down off the jetty and into the boat.

She had no intention of taking the sail-boat out. But, as she remembered the way Zoltán's sensitive fingers had touched the various pieces of equipment in turn, without her being aware of it, her fingers traced those same moves. Oh, how she loved him, oh, how she wanted to stay. Dear Zoltán... Her thoughts had gone on when she suddenly found she was wondering if he was *still* having some intimate conversation with his girlfriend on the telephone—and for some unknown reason she untied the mooring ropes. Jealousy was attacking with a vengeance when, all at once, the dinghy began to move.

Since it had never been her intention to take the boat out, Ella attempted to tie the craft up again, but she gave that up when she all but tipped herself in.

Discretion being the better part of valour, she sat down again, and to start with felt no more than the merest twinge of alarm. Nor when in only seconds the little craft seemed to have bobbed yards away from its mooring was she unduly worried. Perhaps what she needed more than anything just now was something else to concentrate her thoughts on, she mused. And, remembering the effortless way in which Zoltán had manoeuvred the boat, she attempted to do the same—and found that it was far from effortless!

When Ella discovered that, astoundingly, she was some two hundred yards away from the jetty, pure common sense warned that if she didn't want to get herself in some sort of predicament then she had better get herself back to where she'd come from with all speed. There was, she was fast discovering, far more to this sailing business than had at first appeared.

Having decided that it might be a good idea to take half a dozen lessons before going solo, however, Ella then found that with the wind freshening, and the choppiness of the water turning into waves of frightening proportions, to return to the jetty was easier said than done.

A moment later, a gust of fierce wind hit her sail, and, as her small craft was spun crazily about, fear began to enter her heart. She thought of Zoltán, and while she wanted him with her she at the same time knew that as far as he was concerned she was still safely in the house. He most probably had no thought to see her again until breakfast tomorrow morning!

Oh, Zoltán, Zoltán, she thought, and, as the dinghy was hit by another gust of fierce wind and spray hit her face and a frightening wave deposited a vast amount of water into the boat, Ella had the panicky feeling that breakfast-time tomorrow morning would see both her and the boat at the bottom of the lake.

She tried her hardest to think constructively but had an idea that—for all ferries crossed the lake at certain points—motor boats were forbidden, and since she could not see a boat at all she realised that no one knew of her plight. Panic took a stab at her when, recognising that she was in the gravest danger, she was forced to accept that she was in this on her own, and that no one would be coming to her rescue.

It was then that she knew that if she was to survive she was going to have to keep her head. The first thing she must do, she saw, as the wind tore at the sail and took her further and further away from the jetty, was to get that sail down. Then, to add to her problems, the heavens suddenly opened, and the rain poured down.

Ella gritted her teeth, and for the next ten minutes she battled against the forces of nature. But the rope was wet, her hands were wet; in fact, as another wave hit—and not counting the rain or the spray that drenched her the whole time—she was soaked to the skin.

But at last the sail was down and Ella thanked her lucky stars that, although battling against the elements had been exhausting, she was no longer sailing out towards the middle of the lake. What she was, though, was being tossed around as if she and her craft were nothing. Which left her having to hang on like grim death and to bail water out with her hands whenever she had the chance—while hoping with all she had that the little dinghy would not capsize.

She was thinking that she had never imagined that a lake could erupt in the wild way Lake Balaton had, when a wave that was higher than all the rest hit her and made her gasp for breath. It was then that Ella began to sense that she was not going to make it! With the storm growing worse, not lessening, she realised that another wave like that last one could be the finish.

Oh, Zoltán, she thought forlornly, but knew full well that he had no idea where she was. She looked over to where the jetty should have been but she could not even see it—and was on the brink of despair when, on the wind, she heard her name. '...Ella!' she heard the call, 'Ara-bel-la!' Zoltán used to call me Arabella, she thought, and wondered, as she turned in her seat to the sound, if she was going light-headed. She then discovered that she had been looking in the wrong place for the jetty.

It did not surprise her that she had lost her bearings, but she thought she most definitely *had* gone light-headed when, peering through the heavy rain and spray, she thought that she could make out not only the shape of the jetty—but another craft—a craft coming her way!

Hope suddenly surged to new life in her heart, when what seemed an age later she was able to make out that it *was* a craft coming her way—a rowing-boat with a man at the oars pointing the bow of the boat into the waves—it was either that, or be turned over by them.

A different sort of fear entered her heart then, a giant fear—but not for herself. For the man using every atom of his strength at the oars to get to her, the man who was risking his life, to save hers, was Zoltán, the man she loved.

Oh, my darling, she mourned, loving him with all her being and knowing now that it had been Zoltán calling her name—maybe to keep her from despairing—and that it hadn't, as she had thought, been just a sound on the wind.

Be careful! she wanted to shout. Take care! she wanted
to cry. And when a wave hit him and lifted his boat and
she thought it would roll over, Oh, *go back*! she wanted
to scream.

But he weathered that wave, as she somehow managed
to weather the waves that hit her, and slowly, painfully
slowly it seemed in that nightmare of wanting it to be
all safely over, he had rowed, using super-human
strength, she realised, to take her in tow.

Ella took a hurried glance to his grim countenance,
but there was no time then or breath to spare for words.
Just time for a muscle-tearing passing over of rope as,
in terrifying conditions, Zoltán somehow managed to
secure the two craft together. Then he had the bigger
and more impossible task of turning both the boats
around—without capsizing either of them—and of
making back for the nearest land point.

Somehow—though how, when it seemed so impossible?—Zoltán managed to manoeuvre the boats
where he wanted them and was not wasting any time in
rowing for the shoreline.

It seemed a lifetime later, after a ghastly nightmare
world of being buffeted by fierce wind, and assaulted
by more drenching waves, that Ella saw that the shoreline
at last seemed to be closer.

She knew that they were still in danger, but hope leapt
in her heart as Zoltán battled on. Then, with an unexpected suddenness, they hit land, and Oszvald, looking
relieved and anxious at one and the same time, was there
to assist. By then, though, Ella, while feeling totally
exhausted, was such a mass of differing emotions that
she could barely move.

But in moments Zoltán was coming for her. And it
was he—even after the gallant way he had rowed through
such horrendous conditions and must be feeling as if his

arms were wrenched from their sockets—who reached down for her.

Like a child, a trusting child, she stretched up her arms to him and, as he lifted her clear of the dinghy, so she clung to him as though she would never let go.

'Oh, Zoltán!' she cried, and, too distraught to know what she was saying, 'Oh, Zoltán,' she repeated brokenly, and leaning her sodden head against the solid wall of his chest, 'I thought I'd never see you again!' she cried.

But all too soon her haven was gone. For inside a minute Zoltán was putting her unceremoniously from him and was instructing her harshly, 'Go to the house!'

Shaken back to reality by the curt tone of his voice, Ella stared up at him and only then realised that he was in the grip of some formidable emotion too. His face was a chiselled mask giving nothing away, and yet she sensed he was enraged and that his fury was about to break around her head at any moment.

'I'm—s-sorry,' she attempted to apologise for what he must regard as her foolhardiness but saw at once that her apology, as well as being vastly inadequate, was entirely unwanted by him.

'Get into a hot bath at once!' he ignored her to command.

'Zoltán, I——'

'Then come down to the drawing-room!' he gritted.

'Zoltán...' she tried again, but saw that all too obviously she had exceeded all limits, and that he considered he'd wasted enough time on politeness.

He had already started to distance himself from her when, 'The drawing-room in half an hour!' he rapped, and, taking what seemed to her to be a shaken kind of breath, 'I've had *enough*!' he snarled, and, turning, strode furiously from her.

Ella stared after him, then, with the rain still pelting down, she started walking. By the time she reached the house, however, Zoltán was nowhere to be seen, but it was plain that he intended his orders should be obeyed. Because when she had wearily squelched up the stairs to her room it was to discover that Lenke was already at work running her a hot bath, while Frida was on hand to help her out of her waterlogged clothes.

Fifteen minutes later, Ella stepped from her bath and into a warm robe and swiftly began to blow-dry her hair. Soon she would have to go downstairs to face the music, but she did not doubt what form that music would take. Plainly, as Zoltán had said, he'd had *enough*—and that meant enough of *her*.

When it came to making a decision about leaving, Ella knew full well then that she no longer had any choice in the matter. For it was clear to her then that Zoltán intended to throw her out. And, after the way he'd risked his life for her, nor could she say that she blamed him.

CHAPTER NINE

AN ISOLATED sound from somewhere downstairs abruptly penetrated Ella's thoughts, reminding her, when she didn't need reminding, that she was expected elsewhere. It increased her feelings of unease—she didn't want to go down to the drawing-room to be instructed to pack her bags. But, it was now thirty-three minutes since Zoltán had commanded her 'The drawing-room in half an hour' and no amount of her not wanting to meet that fate was going to alter the outcome. Zoltán had been blisteringly angry with her, and the longer she kept him waiting the worse it was going to be.

A minute later Ella left her room, unable to see what could be worse than being thrown out by the man she loved, but realising that she could delay no more. She went down the stairs, having donned a dress of a lovely blue that brought yet more colour to the brilliant blue of her eyes, and faced the fact that all she had left was her pride, and not a great deal of that.

By the time she reached the drawing-room door nerves were beginning to bite with some savagery, but since there were some things which had to be taken on the chin and could not be avoided she composed her features to hide that she was breaking up inside. Then she opened the door, and went in.

Zoltán was there before her looking tall, and every inch a man, and she turned her glance swiftly from him and made renewed efforts to get herself more of one piece. 'I'm sorry if I've kept you waiting,' she managed, looking to him again and noting that he had changed into dry clothes but that he still looked angry enough to want to break her in two. 'I'm sorry too, dreadfully sorry, about—about the boat,' she started to stammer out her apology. 'I mean about t-taking...'

'I credited you with more intelligence!' he sliced her off to snarl stingingly. And, not hesitating to round on her, 'Couldn't you see what the conditions were like out there on the lake?' he demanded, a muscle jerking in his temple as if he was seeing it all over again. Then a furious something in Hungarian left him which she had no chance to comprehend—though she wouldn't have been surprised had he been favouring her with a few Hungarian swear words. 'Didn't you have...?' he began to lay about her again—when her temporarily mislaid spirit spluttered for life.

'I didn't know that it *was* like *that* out there!' she attempted to defend. 'I've looked at the lake many many times and never seen it so, so...'

Words had failed her but not so him. 'Then permit me to inform you *now*, Miss Thorneloe,' he butted in toughly, 'that Lake Balaton has a reputation for suddenly erupting into storms! Six-foot-high waves are not unheard-of out there when it gets going!'

Oh, dear heaven, Ella inwardly gasped, and, for all she didn't think the waves this time had been *that* high, she could only wonder that Zoltán had managed to bring her back at all! But her flattened spirit was dragging itself up from off the ground and, while she was eternally grateful to him for what he had done, she was again starting to grow conscious that she must guard with everything in her that he should not gain so much as a hint of how much he meant to her.

'I—er...' she checked, then, knowing that he'd make mincemeat of her—if she allowed it, 'You should have said, told me before,' she attempted to stand up for herself—but only to have her ears blasted for her trouble, when Zoltán, his grey eyes blazing fiercely, let go with some of his anger.

'I didn't *bloody know* you'd do anything so plain stupid!' he exploded volcanically, equally able to swear in her language as his own when rattled beyond enduring, Ella rapidly realised.

'Yes, well, I'm—sorry,' she repeated her apology, but memory of how terrifying it had been out on the lake took her in its grip again. And, as she recalled the danger Zoltán had put himself in on her account, she knew that the least she owed him was some sort of an explanation. 'I hadn't *meant* to take the boat out,' she told him openly, truthfully. 'My thoughts were miles away when I stepped into the boat...'

'Without meaning to take her out?' he questioned scornfully.

'That's what I said!' she replied with more spirit, stung again, this time because it seemed to her that he was calling her a liar.

'So, go on, you just climbed into the boat—when suddenly it undid its own mooring ropes——'

'*No!*' she denied sharply. 'I did that!' Her brief flurry of anger ebbed as quickly as it had arrived as Ella began to tell him how it had been. 'I was just sort of idly playing about with the ropes, and—er—things,' she went on, starting to feel ridiculous, especially when at his long and direct look, she felt obliged to add a feeble, 'when suddenly the boat started to move.'

'And you thought it would be a good idea to go for a sail?'

'No!' she again denied. 'I told you—I wasn't thinking! My mind was elsewhere and——'

'Too right it was!' he cut in, angry again. Then caught her stone cold when, 'Where?' he questioned abruptly.

Desperately she played for time while she tried to get her thoughts together. 'Where—what?' she asked, and was at once aware, when he seemed to still for a moment, that he knew she was prevaricating—and wondering at the cause.

It was all there in his steady and watchful, 'Your mind was elsewhere,' reminder, and, 'Where was it?' he questioned, his eyes fixed on hers, and all at once Ella felt hot all over.

She needed desperately to come up with some good alternative to the truth—that she hadn't been aware of what she was doing because she had been thinking of her love for him, and how she wanted to stay. She needed urgently to find something other to tell him than the truth that she had been so riven apart by jealousy over Szénia Halász, his lady friend, that she hadn't been aware that she'd undone the dinghy from its moorings, until the boat had started to move.

Suddenly, then, as her quick mind darted off in all directions, she hit on the perfect red herring, and she hurriedly set off on a trail of leading him away from that which he must never know. 'If you must know, I was too busy wondering about my portrait to notice what I was doing.'

'Your—portrait?' he queried slowly, and again, or so it seemed to her, there was a stilled sort of look to him. A sort of stilled look as though he was only then remembering that today was the first time he'd left her alone in his studio.

'Mmm—yes,' she murmured, and, having most satisfyingly drawn him away from one very worrying subject, she was fully prepared to take whatever he threw should he have taken objection to her nosing about his studio in his absence—even if it was supposed to be *her* portrait. 'How could I help but have my mind elsewhere,' she hurried on when, giving away nothing of what he was thinking, Zoltán just stood and coldly stared at her, 'when for weeks now I've been sitting for my portrait, only to discover—er—when you went to take your phone call that you haven't been painting me at all?' Having felt so dreadfully strung up, Ella came to an end, aware that she had been babbling in her nervousness, and only then realised that it might be better if she just shut up altogether.

She dared a flicked glance to Zoltán, but although she had an idea that he was about to make some caustic comment with regard to her vanity barely waiting until his back was turned—though she would have called it curiosity, or interest—he alluded to it not at all. But after another moment of giving her a cold once-over glance— and with no need to use an evading red herring of his own, she was sure, he declared, 'You must be quite exhausted still from your recent battering in the storm,' and, indicating a nearby settee, 'Go and sit down there!' he ordered.

Ella did not take kindly to being bossed about. But this man had just saved her life and she owed him and then some. Also, while she was physically fit enough to be able to bounce back from most energy-draining trials, Zoltán had the ability to make her feel week at the knees in the normal run of things, so she knew that she would welcome something solid beneath her, like a settee, when, as she was aware that he would, he got around to or- dering her out.

Without a word of protest, but knowing that the reason Zoltán hadn't ordered her out yet must be that he intended to give her an almighty rocketing first—and she conceded she'd got that coming—Ella went and sat down on the settee he had indicated.

She was feeling then that no berating words he could hurl at her could in any way be as bad as the final consequence, that of being sent away never to see him again. She looked over to him, to see he had gone to stare out of the window, though she didn't doubt that his mind was busy in selecting just the right words with which to castigate her.

Silently she watched him, but it was when she noticed that he seemed to be under some tremendous strain that, words just seeming to fly from her of their own volition, she spoke first. 'You must be exhausted too!' she exclaimed. 'Much more exhausted than me!' she added, as she remembered—all too vividly—the pure monumental physical energy he'd had to find in order to get them to safety.

His answer was a 'Huh!' kind of grunt which was sufficient to tell her that he'd sit down when he felt like it, and had no need of her belated kind thoughts. It was all there in the way he stayed vertical, and stayed by the window to turn and again stare out.

Oh, how she loved him, Ella thought, and while everything inside urged that she get down on her knees and beg him to allow her to stay a little while longer, still that part of her that was made of sterner stuff got in first and, not waiting to be told 'on your way', 'I'll leave, of course,' she quietly, and with dignity, informed his broad-shouldered back.

But, to her amazement, Zoltán spun round as though she had just shot him, and, 'Leave!' he thundered.

'I...' She faltered, but quickly gathered herself together, to start again, 'Well, naturally, you want me to leave!'

'Like hell I want you to leave!' he roared, his words to Ella seeming to be ripped violently from him as he strode from the window and came to tower angrily over her. 'When did I *ever* indicate that?' he demanded.

In total bewilderment Ella stared up at him. That she leave was a foregone conclusion, she had thought. But, even as her heart began to dance a merry jig at just the thought of being allowed to stay a little while longer, she suddenly twigged the reason. 'Oh—my portrait,' she commented, and realised that Zoltán, despite his heartfelt 'I've had *enough*!' down by the lake, must be appalled at any suggestion that he might break his word—in this case, send her home, her portrait not painted, his promise to her father that paint her he would therefore broken. 'After the way you deliberately risked your life to save me today, my father will have no doubt that you are completely a man of honour,' she quickly stated.

For her trouble she received another 'Huh!' from Zoltán. Though whether he knew what the dickens she was talking about—and she owned that he was making her feel so mixed up that she hardly knew herself—he gave no clue. What she was given, though, was more confusion to cope with when he snarled a short and sharp, 'So you *want* to go!' at her. And, while she reeled from the vehemence in him, 'You can't wait to get back to England to resume your riding with Jeremy Craven, and, no doubt, dancing the night away with David—whoever he might be!'

Flabbergasted by his attack, Ella was not sure her mouth didn't fall open. It was staggering that he had remembered Jeremy's name! But, with Zoltán going for her like that, and while she felt he had every right to have a go at her, she was all the same very much confused to know how Jeremy Craven or her brother David had got into this.

With difficulty, however, she waded her way through the fog, to concentrate on what strangely he seemed to be objecting to the most. 'But—I thought you wanted me to go!' she exclaimed in a sudden rush.

'Go?' he questioned, and unexpectedly took a juddery kind of breath and then, to her utmost bewilderment, and looking straight at her, 'I should want you to go, when my head's so full with schemes and plans to keep you here!' he declared.

Not only did her mouth definitely fall open then, but her eyes went wide, and she wasn't sure that she did not go crimson as a barrage of emotion took her. Zoltán was planning to keep her there!

'I... You...' She wasn't making sense even to herself. But none of what he said was making sense either, so, 'Why?' she finally had to question.

His answer was to take a couple of impatient strides to one of the easy chairs, and, with another impatient movement, push a matching chair close up to the settee she was on. But, when Ella swallowed nervously because it seemed he was going to sit close by her—how was she going to hide her emotions from him that close?—he did not after all sit down. But, as if too het up to be still, he took a few paces from her.

Ella's eyes were on nowhere but him when suddenly he swung back and he barked, 'Surely it's no great news to you that I find you a very appealing woman?' for all the world as though he hadn't an atom of liking for her, she thought. Either that or—as her heart suddenly started vigorously palpitating—or he felt as nervous as she did!

Again she had to swallow, and her eyes had grown saucer-wide when, 'Y-you find me ap-appealing?' she stammered.

'Appealing, attractive, beautiful,' he endorsed. But the harshness had left his voice when he came then and lowered his length into the chair he had pushed near to her, and then revealed, 'I've thought so from the day I first looked at your photograph—I have not changed my opinion.'

Oh, my heavens, Ella thought helplessly, and sorely needed help from somewhere. 'But—you don't like me!' she exclaimed, as she did her level best to keep her feet firmly on the ground. Then she caught Zoltán's alert look on her and could have groaned out loud if he, razor-sharp, had read into that that she would dearly like him to like her; indeed, that it was quite important to her that like her he did.

Her insides were a load of nonsense when, after several long and speculative moments, Zoltán replied, 'Far from disliking you—it is a fact, Arabella, that I've grown to like you more and more with each facet of your character I've come to know.'

'Oh,' she mumbled, and, while her heart idiotically acted the giddy goat, all she could do was to grasp, quite desperately, for a tart note with which to fire, 'If you've grown to like me more and more, then, from your attitude of late, I'd say that you didn't like me at all at the start.'

'Remind me to have a few words with you some time about your acid tongue,' he commented, not unkindly, even a shade humorously, she thought. But, as her heart continued to bang away against her ribs, she observed that there was a much warmer look in his eyes for her as he questioned, 'Should I take heart that you've noticed I haven't been myself this past couple of weeks?'

But that was too much of a leading question as far as Ella was concerned, and she just stayed dumb and stared at him. And after staring back at her lovely blue eyes for some moments Zoltán seemed to relent.

'Forgive that I want so much,' he murmured, 'am impatient for so much, yet have not done you the courtesy of explaining anything.'

You don't have to explain anything, her pride would have her reply. But he did! She wanted to know everything that there was to know—starting with the fact that if, as he said, he had grown to like her more and more, why then had he lately taken more often than not, to acting like a boar with a sore head whenever she was around? But while she could hold down on the pride which would have seen her telling him he didn't have to explain anything, it was that same pride which prevented her from inviting him to please explain everything that he would.

So, again, she stayed quiet, and after long moments of just looking at her Zoltán began on the courtesy he seemed to think he owed her. 'Your father sent a picture of you, and I thought you the most beautiful woman I had ever seen,' he raised her to the heights—only to drop her speedily down, when he added, 'Which makes me more than brainless that I was then prepared to dislike you, and everything I thought you were.'

'How—nice!' she murmured with more than a hint of the acid he had spoken of. It was a wonder to her that he had agreed to paint her at all!

'Perhaps I deserved that,' he accepted, but then confided, 'In my early days of painting portraits, I had many beautiful women sit for me. But frequently I discovered that the beauty was only skin deep.'

For a panicky moment or two as she recalled Zoltán saying something about being allowed time to know his subject, Ella wondered fearfully how close he had looked beneath the surface of her. Had he seen how much she cared for him? Oh, dear heaven, no! She hurried away from such unthinkable thought, and, even while she was aware of the travelling he'd done in his work, 'You—er—had your other—these ladies staying in your home too?' she questioned.

'Never one!' he replied promptly, and, with a long and level look to her, 'You, Arabella,' he asserted, 'always were different.'

That warm look was there in his eyes again, and it was all she could do not to give a nervous gulp. 'I—was?' she asked, staring at him as though mesmerised.

'But of course,' he replied, just as though there was no doubt about it. Though since it was plain she had no idea how she should be so different, he leaned a little forward in his chair, and with his eyes searching hers, he began to clarify, 'I no longer paint portraits. Yet within a short while of seeing your photograph I was agreeing that paint you I will.'

Ella forbore to mention that so far as she was aware, and despite the hours she had spent 'sitting', he hadn't yet started on her picture! But that there was something mighty peculiar about the fact that she had 'sat' for nothing did not seem such an important issue just then.

'You—er—told my father to send me to you,' she took up quietly.

'And, while waiting impatiently for you to arrive, spent the waiting time convincing myself that you'd be without inner beauty.'

'You ... But you couldn't have been all that impatient for me to arrive!' she objected—with this interview going along hugely contrasting lines than she'd imagined— somehow managing to remember that she had telephoned Zoltán on her first night in Budapest. 'I rang you from my hotel the night I arrived, but you were in no hurry to see me!'

'I was in shock.'

'Shock!'

'I was stunned,' he disclosed. 'Wanting to see you, yet suddenly afraid you'd be as I imagined—with no inner beauty. I'd convinced myself too, that you'd have a screechy voice. But what do I hear...' he broke off, and the merest trace of a smile began to curve his mouth '...but that you have a very lovely voice.'

'Oh!' she exclaimed shakenly, loving his mouth, loving him, and making desperate efforts to get herself collected. 'You—er—sound very much as if you were determined to dislike me from the start,' she managed with as much asperity as she could muster.

'I confess, I tried,' he admitted quietly.

'But—why?' she asked, and was in some bewilderment. 'I know I was reluctant to have my portrait painted, and that I dragged my feet in coming to Hungary, but I hadn't otherwise done anything to make you want to dislike me.'

'Had you not, my dear?' he questioned, and, while that alien 'my dear' on his lips sounded not alien at all, and caused her to look at him in some speechlessness, 'It was sufficient that you started off emotions in me the strength of which I would never have believed myself capable.'

Her eyes shot wide. 'Er—really?' she asked unsteadily, and, her eyes glued to him, 'What did I do?'

'To start with, you didn't have to do anything,' he readily admitted, his eyes feasting on her expression, on her face. 'I saw a picture of you—and couldn't get you out of my head.'

'No!' she gasped.

'Oh, but yes,' he contradicted. 'Of course, I scoffed at myself, for I am a man of thirty-six years, and this is plain ridiculous that I am suddenly an insomniac with a penchant for checking the times of flights from England during my insomniac night hours.'

'Good—heavens!' Ella whispered faintly, and while her heart thundered away she began to think that it would never beat normally ever again, 'S-so, because—because I gave you in—er—insomnia, you decided to dislike me.'

'To *try* to dislike you,' he corrected. 'For how could it be that a man of my years should feel so over a woman he had seen only a photograph of, but whom he had never met?' Ella stared at him and would dearly have loved to hear more of what he 'should feel so', but she did not have the nerve to ask, she discovered, and then the moment was lost, for he was going on, 'The cure, I soon decided, was to meet you. Then, I was confidently certain, I would see that it was your beauty only that I was taken with—that your true self would soon show through—and I would once again know what it was to have a sound night's sleep.'

Ella at once wanted to question that 'taken with' but, as before, fear, shyness, she knew not what, held her back. 'So, you—er—agreed to paint my portrait?' she questioned instead.

He nodded, his eyes still as steady as ever on hers. 'I did, and you arrived, and that,' he said succinctly, 'was when my troubles really began.'

'That next day—you rang and ordered me to come to you,' Ella easily recalled.

'And you showed exactly what you thought of my orders by taking your time in coming to me!' said the man whom she was fast realising had missed not a thing.

'You—er—said that your troubles really began then,' she thought to quickly remind him, feeling much too vulnerable suddenly.

'So they did,' he confirmed. 'There was I, quietly positive before I met you that after a few sittings I would have discovered enough of you to be able to happily, and speedily, send you on your way back to England. But, having met you, what do I find but that the more I see of you, the more I need to see of you? And, because of that need, what I am doing is delaying starting these sittings, so that I can keep you here with me the longer.'

What was he *saying*? Ella could hardly think straight any more. But even while she was counselling herself that he couldn't be saying that he... cared for her—could he?—she was striving desperately for calm. 'You needed to get to know your—er—subject better, I think you said,' she stated, her head just then so full of what he was now voicing that she wouldn't have been at all surprised had she misquoted him.

'A lot of good getting to know more of you did me!' he replied with some feeling. 'My theory,' he elucidated, 'just didn't work.'

'Theory?'

'To get you out of my head I set about proving that you were some lightweight. Only, far from proving that you were the awful spoiled female I had supposed—I discovered very early on that you were the most delightful woman of my acquaintance. In no time, that first evening at dinner in actual fact,' he went on, his eyes on hers refusing to let her look away, 'I found that I liked so much about you. Your pride, your good manners towards my housekeeper—the list, little one,' he said softly, 'is endless.'

'Oh—Zoltán,' Ella breathed chokily, and, whether it was something in her eyes, her look, her fear, her hope, she knew not what, but suddenly he had stretched forward to take a hold of her hands.

Then, all at once, it seemed as if he was under some great strain beyond enduring, for he leaned that bit closer and, as if he desperately needed some encouragement from her, 'My dear,' he breathed, 'kiss me, if you want me to go on.'

Perhaps it was just as well that he had not asked for encouragement in words, for she suddenly felt too consumed by emotion to say so much as another word. Then she became aware of the sudden growing intensity of Zoltán's grip on her hands, and, unbelievable as it seemed, she had the craziest idea that he was a man at the end of his tether, and that if she didn't soon kiss him he would walk from the room, from her—and from her life.

It was her turn to grip his hands then, and grip them hard as she sought for courage, and when that courage suddenly arrived she moved that little bit closer to him. Then, tilting her head, she leaned forward and touched a whisper of a kiss to his warm waiting and wanting mouth.

'Arabella!' he cried as her lips left his. The next she knew was that he had left his chair, and was on the settee beside her. And that small salute she had given him was being repaid when he placed his giving mouth gently over hers. 'Forgive my impatience,' he requested softly. 'I know I should have waited, told you everything—explained more fully. But, dear, dear Arabella, my emotions are shot. Seeing you out in that storm, and in a boat that looked about to capsize at any moment was the most terrifying experience of my life and...' he broke off to take a long steadying breath '...I'm nowhere near over it yet,' he confessed.

'I'm sorry, so sorry,' Ella quickly told him, and felt the warmth of his hands holding hers again.

'And I'm sorry too,' Zoltán replied, explaining, at her look of enquiry, for he, in her book, had nothing to apologise for, 'for all those times I was sharp and disagreeable—and going off my head with jealousy.'

'Jealousy!' she exclaimed. 'You've been jealous?'

'From that very first evening you were under my roof,' he replied, and as she stared at him, wide-eyed and disbelieving, 'We were having dinner and everything was going fine, then suddenly you were talking about starting work—and I was convinced there was some man in England that you wanted to hurry home to.'

'Oh, Zoltán,' she sighed, hardly daring to believe what was happening but with no intention of backing away. Indeed, her confidence growing all the time, she felt ready to rush out and grasp with both hands, whatever might transpire. 'There's no man in England I want to hurry home to.'

For her honesty, Ella was rewarded with something spoken very tenderly in Hungarian, which, when accompanied by the most beautiful kiss to her mouth, could, she was certain, only be an endearment. 'My sweet Arabella.' He switched to her language—and as he pulled back from her he confessed, 'That night, that first night you were under my roof when I for the first time in my life suffered insane pangs of jealousy, I knew that I had to take myself from under that same roof in order to get things into perspective.'

'You went out,' she recalled without having to think about it.

'I looked in on a party I'd been invited to,' he told her freely, 'but I had you in my mind the whole time. Then when I could barely wait to see you at breakfast the next morning, you were in turn making me angry by trying to order me to start work straight away, and——'

'I'm sure I never...' she tried to interject, but, at the teasing smile that came to his expression, she broke off.

'In turn you made me angry,' he resumed after a moment, 'and enchanted me when, with your astonishing blue eyes flashing, you got angry too. You called me a temperamental artist,' he recalled, 'and added to the growing list of things I liked about you the fact that you could so easily swing my mood to laughter.'

'I *thought* I heard you laugh!'

'Forgive me—nobody had ever called me a temperamental artist before.'

Ella stared at him for long loving moments, then it popped into her head to mention, 'I thought you despised me because I didn't have a job.'

'Didn't have a job!' he exclaimed in some amazement. 'From what I've so far gathered, and I probably only know half of it, you haven't any time left with which to take on a paid job.'

'Oh, my father wouldn't let me anyhow—take paid work I mean. It was a particularly sore point with me.'

A marvellous grin suddenly appeared on Zoltán's mouth which she found utterly fascinating, the moment before he confidently murmured, 'I'm sure you acquainted your parent, most thoroughly, with your views on the subject.'

'You could say that,' she laughed, her head going slightly back as the musical sound left her. She stilled suddenly, though, when she became aware that as Zoltán looked at her laughing mouth his grin had vanished.

Her laughter vanished too, but while she suddenly knew fear at what he might say next, what he did say caused her eyes to grow wide with shock. For, to her utter astonishment, she heard him say, his voice all gravelly, and as if the words were wrenched from him, 'Oh, Arabella, my darling, is it any *wonder* that I love you?'

Hardly daring to believe her ears, she stared and just stared at him, and saw then the gentle, tender look of love on his face. 'You . . .' she tried, but her voice came out all croakily and she had to break off to clear it, then, 'You—love me?' she asked huskily.

'Is that not what I've been telling you all this while?' he enquired.

'Oh!' she said, and saw the swift look of consternation that crossed his features.

'You misunderstood me when I asked you if you wanted me to go on?' he asked quickly, and Ella was not sure that he hadn't lost some of his colour.

'Oh, no!' she as quickly set him straight. 'I mean, I wanted you to l-love me, b-but I couldn't think that you did.'

'You wanted me to love you?' He quickly mastered his alarm to pick out what was important to him.

Ella felt sorely in need of something steadying as his intent grey eyes burned into hers as he waited for her answer. 'Yes,' she said at last, 'I did.'

'Why?' The word was sharp, as though he was in urgent need of an answer.

'You know why.'

'So tell me.'

'Because—because I—feel the same way,' she answered on a breath of a sound.

'As I love you, and am in love with you,' he encouraged, 'you love me, Arabella?'

'Oh, Zoltán,' she cried, his look, his love, all there urging her on. 'Oh, yes, yes,' she told him, 'I love you—so very much.'

For about a second Zoltán continued to look deeply into her eyes. Then a smile gradually started to appear in his expression, he let go of her hands and gathered her up in his arms. 'My love,' he breathed reverently, and kissed her.

Ella was still close in his embrace when he drew back from her to explore her face and then to kiss her and hold her and keep her near his heart. Ella wound her arms tight around him, hardly daring to breathe lest this all be a dream and the least sound might make it all vanish.

But it was no dream, and Zoltán was again feasting his eyes on her face when he murmured, 'Is it any wonder that my heart should pound the way it's pounding now when I walked into that room and first saw you? Is it any wonder that as I waited for you to join me for dinner that night I should grow so impatient to see you that I came up to get you, pretending I'd forgotten to tell you we would dine at eight.'

'You knew Frida had told me!'

'Of course!' he admitted. 'I was in love with you, and, while trying to discount it, I was having a hard time in coping with it.'

'You loved me *then*!' she exclaimed, and was still trying to take it in as she added, 'I thought you didn't like me?'

'Not like you! My dear, I was in love with you before I ever met you.'

'You fell in love with my photograph?' she asked, amazed.

'I couldn't believe it either,' he smiled, 'which is why I fought with all I could against it. It was quite preposterous, I thought. Yet before long, and much before you had so much as begun to sit for me, I was discovering that your beauty was not just an outer layer—but that you are beautiful through and through. That you are in fact just quite adorable!'

'You think...' Her voice tailed off, her heart positively singing that he should think so of her. 'I never so much as guessed!' she found her voice to exclaim.

'You weren't supposed to,' he replied lovingly.

'Because you were still trying to discount it yourself?' she queried with what brain-power she was left with—just to know that Zoltán loved her was making her head spin.

'Discounting, denying,' he agreed, going on, 'You arrived at my home one Friday, yet by Sunday, while I'm still denying what my heart is telling me, I found that I—who had always held the truth in much esteem—was lying like a professional when I invented to you the idea that Frida suffers from rheumatism.'

'You mean she doesn't?' Ella asked startled.

'Not so much as a twinge.'

'But—but why say she has if——?'

'My dear love, can't you see yet how it is with me? I wanted some time alone with you but, in those early days of learning to cope with and hide my emotions for you—emotions which I just couldn't allow myself to trust—I felt it better to be alone with you, but not alone in my studio.'

'Alone with me, but in a crowd, you mean?'

He nodded, 'I've had quite a desperate time of it, my dear,' he revealed. 'Disbelieving it was possible to fall in love with a photograph, then meeting you, realising from the way you would flare up at me that you were more ready to hate than love me, but so wanting to be with you that I told my housekeeper not to disturb us over breakfast that Sunday morning.'

'And subsequently invented her bout of rheumatism,' Ella smilingly put in.

'And when I was still trying to deny this crazy thing that had happened to me, discovered to my astonishment that you were—are—a wonderful caring person who was fully prepared to take over my housekeeper's duties if it would save her pain!'

'Anyone would,' she replied, and, as Zoltán looked most sceptical about that statement, 'But, if Frida didn't have rheumatism, she must have thought it most odd when you told her that I'd cook dinner that evening!' she suddenly exclaimed, remembered how Zoltán had translated her offer into Hungarian for her.

'She might have, had I told her anything but that you and I would be having lunch and dinner out that day.'

At her look of surprise, Zoltán, as if unable to resist it, kissed her, and held her tightly in a warm embrace, and, as his ardour grew, Ella forgot everything. She was still a little under the influence of amnesia when he broke the kiss and stared lovingly into her slightly flushed face.

'Um...' she said, as she tried to get her thoughts together, and, 'You kissed me that night,' she murmured dreamily, and knew she must be all over the place when from somewhere she remembered how Zoltán had told her that Oszvald was an excellent cook, and, 'Is Oszvald the excellent cook you told me he was?' she found herself asking.

'I've absolutely no idea,' Zoltán replied, his eyes twinkling, though to her relief he was remarkably tuned in to her wavelength. 'And yes,' his expression was all at once serious, 'I did kiss you that night. You were stunning in your green dress, your gorgeous red hair cascading over your shoulders. The whole evening had been fantastic. Is it any wonder that my self-control was in pieces, or that the moment we touched I should want to take you in my arms?'

'I'd—um—never—been kissed like that before,' she admitted shyly.

Tenderly he dropped a light kiss on her brow, and then, looking oh, so lovingly down at her, 'You said something similar at the time,' he murmured. 'I knew by then that you were a virgin and were to be protected.

Which,' he added, 'made it essential that I find some self-control, and quickly. You, my darling,' he breathed softly, 'had responded superbly, yet I feared to take you in my arms again—for it seemed then that I must protect you—against me!'

'Oh, Zoltán,' she whispered warmly, and was gently kissed again.

Some moments later he pulled back from her to quietly tell her, 'That Sunday had been marvellous for me. At lunch you'd delighted me by showing interest enough to ask me personal questions, and I'd seen you eager and alive in my company. The day was crowned when I held you, responsive, in my arms. Small wonder then that by Monday I had acknowledged to myself that I loved you with all my being. But while at the same time I was so all over the place in my head—this situation new to me— I had to swiftly hide my love when it became plain, at breakfast, that you were most clearly regretting that we'd embraced.'

'It wasn't that I was regretting it,' Ella rushed to tell him. 'And I hadn't meant to be unpleasant at all. It was just that—well, nerves, I think.'

'Sweet love,' he crooned, 'I could have made things better for you, couldn't I? But by then I was half regretting my promise to paint you. Things,' he declared, 'were not working out the way I'd planned. You, according to my calculations, should have been totally self-centred, and idle. But you're not. You're sensitive and lovely, and I just don't know where the hell I am any more.'

'Oh, my dear,' she cried huskily, and adored the smile he gave her as he went on,

'Can you wonder that I decided I needed to find some aggression? This impudent woman who was demanding whether I was going to start work on her portrait that day would be walking all over me—if I allowed it.'

'You thought that!' she gasped, her confidence soaring; Zoltán, the man she loved, loved her—what else mattered? 'Tell me more?' she asked, her smile matching his.

'So, I decided we would come here, to the lake,' he obliged, 'and decided also, since just looking at your lovely tantalising mouth when I brought your luggage to your room was enough to confirm that my self-control was still ready to fracture at any time, that I'd better involve myself with work entirely unconnected with you.'

'You were busy for a whole week,' Ella recalled.

'And still, for all my self-lectures on self-control, experiencing very worrying moments of weakness when you were near,' he asserted. 'Though it was a week after our arrival here when, back in my studio after lunch that particular Monday, I began to think I'd been too tough on you. I couldn't work for thinking that I might have hurt your feelings, and came looking for you.'

'Ah!' Ella exclaimed. 'That was the day I went for a ride on Oszvald's bike.'

'So I discovered.'

'And were angry with me?'

'Not to begin with,' he denied. 'To start with I was amused when I learned from Oszvald that you'd borrowed his cycle. I can recall thinking, "Oh, the lovely darling," as I got the car out to come looking for you.'

'Honestly!' She saw the truth of what he was saying in his expression. Then, that day pictured most vividly in her mind, 'Your amusement soon changed when you found me,' she reminded him—a touch impishly.

But she saw at once that he needed no reminding, nor had he forgotten a thing. 'You were drinking brandy with some other man, *and* laughing with him—well, smiling,' he amended. 'I, my dear love, found that very far from amusing! Nor was there any way I was going to stand for it!'

'You accused me of picking up men in bars,' she recalled.

'I must beg your pardon for that,' he stated sincerely.

'I'll forgive you anything,' she told him happily.

'Even though you were most definitely furious at the time? From the way you slammed out of my car, I was convinced you'd gone straight to your room to pack.'

'I did.'

'*You did*!'

'Well—I got my suitcases out. And then...' Her voice tailed off.

'And then?' Zoltán pressed. 'Please tell me, my love, I want you to feel that you can tell me anything now. No secrets.'

'It was my greatest secret,' Ella murmured. 'I was so angry I didn't care a button that my father would create like the devil when I got home. Then, while I was—forgive me—still mentally calling you a few unpleasant names—it suddenly hit me that I just couldn't leave.'

'Couldn't?'

'Couldn't—because—I was in love with you.'

'You were in... You knew then!'

Ella nodded. 'I was shattered,' she confessed, then thought for a moment, and then owned, 'Though I suppose there had been quite a few signs along the way.'

'You're not going to hold back on me now, are you?' Zoltán asked, when it seemed she would do that very thing.

'Wouldn't dream of it.' She smiled, and somehow, they mutually kissed.

'Signs?' he prompted.

'Ah, yes.' Ella got herself back together. 'Well, for a start, no man had ever disturbed my emotions as much as you did. I was all churned up about you at my hotel and that was before I'd met you,' she recalled.

'And?'

'And you have the power to make me more angry than any man I've ever met. And while that doesn't sound very loving, I know, it goes a long way to show that you have a knack of disrupting my otherwise fairly calm self.'

'Don't stop there!' he ordered, and she laughed, simply because she couldn't help it.

'Then one day,' she complied, 'you told me that the lake freezes in December, and I was quite staggered to realise that I wanted to still be here then.'

'You did?' he questioned, and his expression was stern, serious, and as though a confirming answer would mean a great deal to him.

'Oh, yes,' she beamed.

'And I was so afraid all the time that you would leave—especially after your fury that particular day. I vowed then that I'd control myself better, that I'd try and get you to forgive me by being on my best behaviour,' he admitted, continuing, as she stared, her eyes shining with love to him, 'Yet that same evening, even while I was in the middle of laughing at something you'd said, I suddenly broke into a cold sweat—because I felt on the edge of revealing my true feelings. But—what if I did? What if I told you—and ruined everything. What if you straight away flew back to England. I knew then that I had to be on my own.'

'Oh, Zoltán!' she cried tenderly, and, touching a hand to his face, had that hand captured, and kissed, and was having to fight hard to recall, 'So—you—told me to have an early night—that you were starting work on my portrait in the morning.'

'And, while I enjoyed every enchanting moment of being across the room from you in my studio,' he took up, 'I should have realised before I started that to attempt to massage the knots out of your stiffened muscles was a mistake.'

'Things did—er—get out of hand very quickly,' Ella contributed.

'Out of hand!' he exclaimed. 'My dear, just to touch your skin set me on fire. I just had to kiss you. Then, while I was fighting with all I had to not kiss you again, you offered me your lips—and I, until your shyness overcame you—forgot everything. My darling Arabella,' he murmured, 'is it any wonder that, with my control hanging by a very frail strand, I have been afraid to touch you again? You, my dear,' he told her with a gentle smile, 'have a chemistry which I find electrifying.'

'I'm—er—rather glad about that,' she laughed, and as a grin at her sauce chased across his features, and made her heart renew its pounding, 'Is that why you didn't come to the dining-room for lunch that day?' she asked.

'I tried to keep away from you,' he admitted, 'but only to wonder, as I ate my solitary lunch in my studio, could you, apart from an understandable shyness, have responded so freely had you no liking for me at all?'

'What did you decide?'

'My head was, and has been, too much of a morass for me to decided anything other than that I wanted to see you. So, I came looking for you.'

'And found me down on the jetty—and took me for a sail.'

'Do you mind if we don't talk about sailing just now?' he asked quietly, and Ella guessed that, while she had made great strides in getting over some of the trauma of what had so recently happened when she'd gone solo sailing, Zoltán was still having some horror about it.

'All right,' she agreed instantly. 'So we came back after something I'd enjoyed and,' she thought a spot of teasing might lighten things for him, 'you had to be beastly and spoil it all for me.'

'It was your fault for reminding me of your brandy-drinking friend when you asked me about Oszvald's cycle,' Zoltán growled.

And Ella laughed. 'Oh, I do love you,' she murmured shyly, and adored it when Zoltán pulled her close, and began kissing her.

It was many minutes later, though it seemed like only seconds, when he pulled back and breathed throatily, 'For the sake of my sanity, not to mention the trust your father has placed in me, I think we'd better talk some more.'

'Shame!' Ella declared wickedly, and was consumed with laughter when,

'Oh, do I have a score to settle with you!' Zoltán promised. But, after another minute of saying nothing but seeming as if he was trying hard to remember what it was they had been talking about, 'To get back to your brandy-drinking friend—you've no plans to see him again, I hope?'

'Certainly not!' she said firmly.

'Then—how about...Jeremy Craven?' he questioned, all sign of good humour suddenly gone from his expression.

'Jeremy is a good friend, and nothing more,' Ella quickly assured him.

'You go riding with him.'

'His family have a few horses. They're glad of anyone who can ride to exercise them.'

'Hmph,' Zoltán grunted. 'You go dancing with him too!' he documented.

'That's true, but seldom alone. I've girlfriends too.' Ella went on, 'There's a crowd of us. We sort of grew up together.'

Zoltán was silent for a moment. Then, 'And David—the one who telephoned?' And before she could reply, 'From what I heard, it sounded as though you couldn't wait to get back to England!'

'David,' she quickly assured him, 'is my brother.'

'Your *brother*!' For a few moments Zoltán stared at her in some stupefaction. Then, 'Have you any idea what I've been through, woman?' he demanded. Though there was a self-derisory humour in his look, and some relief, when, 'If it wasn't thoughts of *Timót* and how I was going to prevent you seeing him again, then thoughts of you and your regular boyfriend Jeremy Craven were gnawing away at me. And if that wasn't enough, I've been driven mad since Friday wondering who the hell this David is that you're so keen to get back to—is it any wonder that our drive to Tihany was a disaster?'

'I'm sorry,' she apologised sweetly, adding honestly, 'I hadn't realised that you didn't know that my brother's name is David. He rang to tell me that he's getting married next month and to say that he'd like me there.'

'Hmm,' Zoltán grunted, then, a little stiffly, she thought, 'You still prefer I should not know the trouble he is in?'

'No!' she denied.

'You said it was a family matter,' he reminded her.

'I offended you—I'm so sorry,' she immediately apologised.

'I felt shut out—when I desperately wanted to be included in everything that concerns you,' he owned.

'Oh, I wish I'd known!' she cried, and quickly set about making matters right by explaining. 'Actually, I was more trying to cover up my feelings than trying to shut you out.'

'How so?' he enquired, clearly puzzled, and Ella realised that she wasn't explaining it very well at all.

'It was yesterday.' She made another stab at it. 'I was on the couch in the studio and feeling quite downcast at the thought that you would never care for me when suddenly you asked me if something was wrong. Well, I couldn't tell you the truth, could I?'

'I wish you had, my dear love,' he murmured and gently kissed her.

'Well, anyway,' Ella surfaced, 'er—I invented that I was wondering if the trouble at home was over—and then found, because it is all over, that I couldn't continue to lie to you.'

'That I like,' Zoltán grinned.

And Ella grinned too as she revealed, 'For the record, all hell broke loose at home when a Mr Edmonds rang to tell my father that he was coming at once to see him—and David confessed that Mr Edmonds' daughter was expecting his baby.'

'Ah!' Zoltán exclaimed. 'So now everything is resolved, with David about to marry Mr Edmonds' daughter,' and, with a superb smile curving his superb mouth again, 'and I can only be so very glad, sweet love, that all hell broke loose.'

'You are?'

'Did it not bring you to me the quicker?' he enquired, having not forgotten it seemed, that but for her brother getting into 'hot water' with her father she would have delayed yet further her arrival in Hungary.

Ella's answer was to reach up and kiss him, and as his arm tightened about her she forgot everything for a while save the touch of his mouth on hers. Then he was murmuring endearments in his own language, and telling her how he would show her his country, and, as her heart beat erratically at the happy prospect of touring his country with him, 'You'll show me Tihany again?' she asked.

'It will be my pleasure to show you Tihany again,' he agreed, his eyes tender on her. 'Though our first visit was only one desperate measure of not depriving myself of your company; I needed an alternative to having you across the room from me when, just by looking at you, the urge to take you in my arms became near unbearable.'

'Truly!' Ella gasped.

'Very truly,' he replied. 'But that wasn't the first time that the urge to take you in my arms became too much.' And, while she stared at him wide-eyed, 'Those were the times when I *did* have to deprive myself of your company. Times when I invented that the light was bad, and, occasionally, when the urge to hold you close to my heart grew so overwhelming, that I had to take myself out of the house entirely, and eat my dinner elsewhere.'

'Oh, Zoltán!' she whispered. Then, when all he had so far said had gone to build layer upon layer of belief in the unbelievable—that he actually did love *her*—so, Ella found that she suddenly had the complete confidence she needed to ask that which, at times, had torn her apart.

'You want to ask me something, sweet love, I can see it in your face.' Zoltán was there to help her out when she was having difficulty getting started.

'Well, yes, actually,' she agreed.

'So?' he encouraged further, his look gently waiting. 'No secrets—remember.'

'Um—can I ask—those nights you dined out—er—without me...?'

'Yes?' he smiled more encouragement.

'Did you—dine alone?' There it was—out!

'You thought I was dining with some lady?' he enquired, and, as the notion took root, 'You've been jealous too?' he asked in delight.

Ella guessed it only fair that he should be pleased at the notion; lord knew she found his jealousy comforting. Though, for answer, she gave him just one name. 'Szénia Halász,' she drew out of the dark depths—and was astonished at his reaction.

'It worked!' he exclaimed with some relish. 'I didn't think it had but...' He broke off. 'Forgive me, my dear, but with my emotions so mercurial where you're concerned I took quite some heart that you once showed interest enough to ask about the women in my life. I'll admit though, only to feel utterly deflated, when, I having given you Szénia Halász's name, you appeared to care not an iota.'

'I,' Ella quietly revealed, 'have been the deepest green with jealousy.'

'Truly?' he joyfully bounced her word back at her, and Ella just had to laugh.

She was still smiling when, 'Truly,' she replied. Though her smile faded when she asked solemnly, 'Do you still see her?' and for long tormenting moments suffered Zoltán's steady gaze on her.

Then, 'Yes,' he confessed, 'I do,' but as she stiffened in his hold he quickly added, 'Would you wish it that, because I love and adore you and have given you my whole heart, I should refuse to speak to my great-aunt Szénia when she phones?'

'Your gr... You—*wretch*!' Ella exploded. But, as relief washed over her, 'You—wonderful, wonderful wretch,' she added lovingly.

'I love you,' he whispered, and kissed her lightly on the mouth and then asked, 'Forgive me, my love, but it has been an enormous strain for me.'

'For you too?' She swiftly forgave him.

'Hell isn't understating what I've been through—once thinking I saw a look of love in your eyes, and then being certain it was all part of this agony I'm having to endure. Then starting to feel afraid that you'd see how my day starts and ends with you. Masking that, but only to begin to read that you want to leave in everything you say. Yet, even when I'm sure you can't care for me—I cannot bear to let you go.' He touched his mouth gently to hers, and then went on, 'So much so, sweet Arabella, that when my great-aunt, who lives in Budapest, rang here for me to tell the family that she'd been admitted to hospital after a fall, I was in no time making plans to take you to Buda with me at once—thereby hoping to delay your departure for another few weeks.'

'You . . .' Her mouth fell open, and several questions presented themselves to her at the same time. 'Your great-aunt—she's all right?' she decided to ask first.

'An X-ray has revealed she has a broken hip, she told me, though I afterwards rang the surgeon and he says that, although he will have to operate, it is a straight-forward operation.'

'You will go and see her today?'

'This evening,' Zoltán assured her. 'She will be in the operating theatre in an hour from now, so there is little point in going straight away. Not, of course, that I was going to tell you that,' he smiled.

'You were planning, for me to go to Budapest with you—at a moment's notice—and then to delay the work on my picture for various reasons?'

'I was planning to delay your departure from Hungary for as long as I could,' he admitted. 'I came looking for you,' he went on, but, as his grip on her tightened, she realised that he was reliving where it was he had found her. 'I don't know even now why I went down to the jetty, but you weren't in your room and Oszvald said you hadn't borrowed his cycle—then went on about how he'd been checking one of the dinghies over but how when he'd recognised signs that a storm looked due he'd decided to leave it for a while. Then I went down to the jetty—and thank God I did!' he said on a heartfelt sound, but at the raw note in his voice Ella realised that now might be the right time for him to talk any remaining trauma out of his system, so stayed quiet. And after some seconds of Zoltán holding her in a grip as though he would never let her go, he had got himself together again, and was telling her, 'I knew then—when I got you to shore—that I'd had it. That I couldn't take any more.'

Ella again recalled his snarled 'I've had *enough*'. 'You told me to take a hot bath and to be in this room in half an hour,' she inserted quietly.

'And went upstairs myself—but only to have the most staggering lightning-bolt of a thought strike me as I was getting into some dry clothing.'

'What was that?' she asked, and was kissed on both cheeks for her trouble.

'I was re-living again the nightmare of it,' he revealed. 'Then re-living the way, once I'd got you safe again, you'd clung to me.'

'You guessed—that I had some feeling for you?'

'Not at all,' he denied. 'You'd had one hell of a scare. To my way of thinking after such a scare you'd have clung to just about anyone who'd come and got you. Yet, as I then stopped to go over every word we'd exchanged, I clearly remembered how you'd held on to me and said how you thought you would never see me again.

And, while that too could all have been part of the fright
you'd had, I all at once realised that you knew that it
wasn't just anyone you were clinging to. You'd called
my name, clung on to *me* in fear that you might never
see *me* again.'

'I gave myself away.'

'You gave me near heart failure. Did that mean what
I thought, and hoped, that it meant?'

'You thought it did?'

'I thought—knew that I had to find out. That it had
to be all, or nothing. And that, were it nothing, I would,
from somewhere, have to find the will to send you back
to England.'

'Oh, darling!' she cried, and he seemed to like the
word on her lips for him, for he held her close up to
him and again she clung to him. 'I haven't thanked you
for saving my life,' she murmured huskily against his
throat.

'Thanks be damned,' he growled. 'I was saving my
own life—don't you know yet that there is no life for
me without you?'

'Dear Zoltán,' she cried, and held on to him for long
minutes until gradually the intense emotions of the
moment started to ebb, and she searched for something
with which to lighten the mood. She pulled back to look
at his face, and thought she had found that light note
she wanted when, 'You'd have sent me back to England
without my portrait started?' she attempted to tease.

'Started?' he queried, and his superb mouth curving
upwards, 'Sweet love, it's finished.'

'*Finished*!'

'And has been for some time.'

'But—but—you've never shown it to me! Time and
time again I've had to hold back from asking for a look
at it! When can I see it?' she asked eagerly.

'And there was I thinking you were totally without curiosity,' he teased her this time.

'I didn't want to be like your other sitters if...' Her voice tailed off as an inconsequential thought jumped into her head. 'Do you always massage the shoulders...?' She broke off when she saw it looked as though Zoltán was about to burst out laughing.

'You were the only one,' he replied, and was all at once getting to his feet, and bringing her to her feet too. 'By the time you arrived in Hungary I had sketched you so many times from your photograph I could have done it blindfold,' he said looking down at her. 'Which is probably half the reason why I'd got your picture finished long before I wanted it to be done.'

'You were working on a landscape, yet kept looking over to me,' she thought to mention, puzzled.

'Can I help it if I like to look at you for the pure joy of it?' he replied.

There was no answer to that. 'I love you,' she told him.

'My darling,' he murmured, and kissed her and then walked a couple of paces across the room with her. There he halted to tell her, 'Sweet Arabella, when I was forced to accept that I might have to let you go I went and collected your portrait from its hiding-place. It's here—waiting for you,' he told her, and with that left her for a moment to go to the back of the other settee in the room, where he bent down to pick something up.

It was her portrait, and Ella could hardly wait while he brought it, as yet only on a wood frame, and propped it up on the settee—and then came over to her, to step to the side of her where he no longer blocked her view of it.

A gasp of wonder left her the moment she caught her first glimpse of the delicately complexioned, utterly beautiful blue-eyed redhead who stared back at her. She was staggered by the eager, alert and slightly impish woman who, with a faint suggestion of a smile on her mouth looked back. An alive woman, but a woman of innocence.

'It's beautiful!' she gasped. 'Is it truly me?'

'It truly is,' he replied. 'Do you not recognise yourself?'

'I'm not sure,' she answered and was shaken to her foundations by his reply.

'Then permit me, my darling Arabella,' he breathed softly, 'to introduce you to a portrait of my future wife.'

'Your future wife!' she exclaimed, spinning from the picture to stare at him.

'You are going to marry me—and soon?' he demanded, his eyes urgently searching hers.

'Oh, yes,' she sighed.

Gently, tenderly, he kissed her, and in the semicircle of his left arm she turned to look at her portrait again. And it was then that she suddenly realised that the beautiful half-smiling redhead who looked back was indeed her—but that there was an extra dimension. And that that extra dimension was that the picture was painted by an artist who was very much in love with the woman in the green velvet dress.

'You do love me, don't you?' she whispered in a shaken kind of voice, and as she raised her head to look at him there was no question there, just the truth of the statement.

'Very much so,' he confirmed, looking down into her shining blue eyes. 'Your father sent me your photograph, and I thought it ludicrous that I should fall in love with a photograph. But I have since realised that it is far more ludicrous that I should meet you and even think to get you out of my heart again.'

'Oh, Zoltán!' she sighed.

'My sweet love,' he breathed, and pulled her closer to him.

OFFICIAL RULES • MILLION DOLLAR SWEEPSTAKES
NO PURCHASE OR OBLIGATION NECESSARY TO ENTER

To enter, follow the directions published. **ALTERNATE MEANS OF ENTRY:** Hand print your name and address on a 3"x5" card and mail to either: Harlequin "Match 3," 3010 Walden Ave., P.O. Box 1867, Buffalo, NY 14269-1867, or Harlequin "Match 3," P.O. Box 609, Fort Erie, Ontario L2A 5X3, and we will assign your Sweepstakes numbers. (Limit: one entry per envelope.) For eligibility, entries must be received no later than March 31, 1994. No responsibility is assumed for lost, late or misdirected entries.

Upon receipt of entry, Sweepstakes numbers will be assigned. To determine winners, Sweepstakes numbers will be compared against a list of randomly preselected prizewinning numbers. In the event all prizes are not claimed via the return of prizewinning numbers, random drawings will be held from among all other entries received to award unclaimed prizes.

Prizewinners will be determined no later than May 30, 1994. Selection of winning numbers and random drawings are under the supervision of D.L. Blair, Inc., an independent judging organization, whose decisions are final. One prize to a family or organization. No substitution will be made for any prize, except as offered. Taxes and duties on all prizes are the sole responsibility of winners. Winners will be notified by mail. Chances of winning are determined by the number of entries distributed and received.

Sweepstakes open to persons 18 years of age or older, except employees and immediate family members of Torstar Corporation, D.L. Blair, Inc., their affiliates, subsidiaries and all other agencies, entities and persons connected with the use, marketing or conduct of this Sweepstakes. All applicable laws and regulations apply. Sweepstakes offer void wherever prohibited by law. Any litigation within the province of Quebec respecting the conduct and awarding of a prize in this Sweepstakes must be submitted to the Régies des Loteries et Courses du Quebec. In order to win a prize, residents of Canada will be required to correctly answer a time-limited arithmetical skill-testing question. Values of all prizes are in U.S. currency.

Winners of major prizes will be obligated to sign and return an affidavit of eligibility and release of liability within 30 days of notification. In the event of non-compliance within this time period, prize may be awarded to an alternate winner. Any prize or prize notification returned as undeliverable will result in the awarding of that prize to an alternate winner. By acceptance of their prize, winners consent to use of their names, photographs or other likenesses for purposes of advertising, trade and promotion on behalf of Torstar Corporation without further compensation, unless prohibited by law.

This Sweepstakes is presented by Torstar Corporation, its subsidiaries and affiliates in conjunction with book, merchandise and/or product offerings. Prizes are as follows: Grand Prize–$1,000,000 (payable at $33,333.33 a year for 30 years). First through Sixth Prizes may be presented in different creative executions, each with the following approximate values: First Prize–$35,000; Second Prize–$10,000; 2 Third Prizes–$5,000 each; 5 Fourth Prizes–$1,000 each; 10 Fifth Prizes–$250 each; 1,000 Sixth Prizes–$100 each. Prizewinners will have the opportunity of selecting any prize offered for that level. A travel-prize option, if offered and selected by winner, must be completed within 12 months of selection and is subject to hotel and flight accommodations availability. Torstar Corporation may present this Sweepstakes utilizing names other than Million Dollar Sweepstakes. For a current list of all prize options offered within prize levels and all names the Sweepstakes may utilize, send a self-addressed, stamped envelope (WA residents need not affix return postage) to: Million Dollar Sweepstakes Prize Options/Names, P.O. Box 4710, Blair, NE 68009.

The Extra Bonus Prize will be awarded in a random drawing to be conducted no later than May 30, 1994 from among all entries received. To qualify, entries must be received by March 31, 1994 and comply with published directions. No purchase necessary. For complete rules, send a self-addressed, stamped envelope (WA residents need not affix return postage) to: Extra Bonus Prize Rules, P.O. Box 4600, Blair, NE 68009.

For a list of prizewinners (available after July 31, 1994) send a separate, stamped, self-addressed envelope to: Million Dollar Sweepstakes Winners, P.O. Box 4728, Blair, NE 68009.   SWP-H12/93

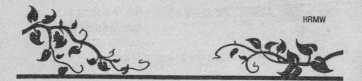

Relive the romance...
Harlequin and Silhouette
are proud to present

by Request™

A program of collections of three complete novels by the most-requested authors with the most-requested themes. Be sure to look for one volume each month with three complete novels by top-name authors.

In September: **BAD BOYS**   Dixie Browning
                                            Ann Major
                                            Ginna Gray

No heart is safe when these hot-blooded hunks are in town!

In October: **DREAMSCAPE**   Jayne Ann Krentz
                                            Anne Stuart
                                            Bobby Hutchinson

Something's happening! But is it love or magic?

In December: **SOLUTION: MARRIAGE**   Debbie Macomber
                                            Annette Broadrick
                                            Heather Graham Pozzessere

Marriages in name only have a way of leading to love....

Available at your favorite retail outlet.

REQ-G2

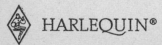

HARLEQUIN®   Silhouette